BATMAN™
RETURNS

MICHAEL
KEATON

DANNY
DeVITO

MICHELLE
PFEIFFER

BATMAN™

RETURNS

WARNER BROS. PRESENTS

A TIM BURTON FILM MICHAEL KEATON

DANNY DeVITO MICHELLE PFEIFFER "BATMAN RETURNS" AND CHRISTOPHER WALKEN

MICHAEL GOUGH PAT HINGLE MICHAEL MURPHY MUSIC BY DANNY ELFMAN CO-PRODUCER LARRY FRANCO

EXECUTIVE PRODUCERS JON PETERS, PETER GUBER, BENJAMIN MELNIKER, MICHAEL USLAN

BASED UPON BATMAN CHARACTERS CREATED BY BOB KANE AND PUBLISHED BY DC COMICS STORY BY DANIEL WATERS AND SAM HAMM

SCREENPLAY BY DANIEL WATERS PRODUCED BY DENISE DI NOVI TIM BURTON DIRECTED BY TIM BURTON

DOLBY STEREO TM & S 1992 DC COMICS INC. READ THE WARNER PAPERBACK SOUNDTRACK ALBUM ON WARNER BROS. CASSETTES AND CDs WARNER BROS.
A TIME WARNER COMPANY

adapted by Andrew Helfer
story by Daniel Waters and Sam Hamm
screenplay by Daniel Waters

Little, Brown and Company

Boston Toronto London

First Edition

ISBN 0-316-17757-1

Library of Congress Cataloging-in-Publication information is available.

10 9 8 7 6 5 4 3 2 1

BUF

Printed in the United States of America

The man paced up and down the hall of his huge mansion. As one of the wealthiest men in Gotham City, he was usually surrounded by advisers and servants, but at this moment he wanted to be alone. His wife lay in one of the rooms at the end of the hall, a doctor and nurse by her side. The man knew that soon he would become a proud father, and his wife a happy mother. For now, all he could do was wait for that moment to arrive.

Then he heard it. The goos and gahs of a baby. The man turned and raced to see his wife and newborn child. Halfway down the corridor, he was met by the nurse, who looked strangely dazed. She hardly seemed to notice the man as she staggered past. A moment later, the doctor emerged from the room. He seemed horrified, as though he had seen a ghost.

1

What could be the problem? the man wondered as he opened the door and peered inside. Then he saw it.

And he screamed.

By Christmas Eve six months later, life had changed for the man and his wife. All their servants had resigned, and the man's many advisers had all decided to conduct their business with him over the phone, rather than at the mansion. The Christmas party the couple planned had been canceled when dozens of their friends called to say they had all suddenly come down with the flu.

But the husband and his wife knew the real reason why their friends and employees had abandoned them. It sat in the metal cage in the middle of their living room, staring through the darkness at them with beady eyes. It was their child, their baby . . . and even *they* could hardly bear to look at it.

But through the bars of the playpen prison, it could look at them. It watched them gulp down martini after martini; watched them shake their heads sadly; watched the mother turn on the radio and listened as she halfheartedly mumbled the words to a cheery Christmas tune:

"He knows when you are sleeping . . . He knows when you're awake . . ."

It listened and watched — until it saw something else . . .

The family cat.

As the husband prepared yet another martini, the wife spotted the cat from the corner of her eye. It slinked across the lushly carpeted floor, moving past the dark metal cage. As it brushed up against the bars, the wife's eyes widened in terror. She tried to shout a warning—but it was too late. In an instant, the cat was yanked inside the cage. From the darkness, husband and wife heard a single feline scream . . . and nothing more.

The unhappy couple looked at each other as they gulped down their martinis. Something had to be done. Tonight.

A light snow was falling on the winding path as the husband and wife grimly walked through Gotham City Park. To the happy family strolling from the opposite direction, the carriage the strange couple pushed along looked like a wicker cage. Could there actually be a child inside that leather-strapped contraption?

"Merry Christmas!" the happy couple chirped.

The husband and wife barely smiled in response. All they could think about was the dreadful task they had to perform. As they walked, they kept glancing over their shoulders, to make sure no one was watching them.

Soon, they came upon a stone bridge — a beautiful storybook affair, with a cheery brook bubbling below. Husband and wife looked at each other for a moment and then, as one, lifted the bizarre baby carriage up and heaved it over the side. As they turned and walked off into the night, the husband and wife prayed they would never see it — or its contents — ever again.

The carriage hit the water, but instead of sinking into the icy depths, it was carried along in the water currents out of the park and into the ancient Gotham City sewer system. Down the murky waters it slid, deeper and deeper through the twisting tangle of tunnels and pipelines. Picking up speed here, slowing down there, the carriage raced along ever-narrowing tunnels, until it was spewed out into an enormous underground cavern.

Here, the water was calm, and a chill colder than Christmas in Gotham City hung in the air. The carriage bobbed along the gentle waves until it came to rest up against a snowy shore. An arctic island, long forgotten in Gotham City. A familiar pair of beady eyes peered out through the carriage bars —

And another pair of beady eyes peered back. Then another pair. And another. Soon four pairs of beady eyes were curiously examining the carriage and its cargo. They were penguins! The creature inside the carriage smiled.

He was home.

Years later ... Gotham Plaza was packed with shoppers and tourists. The department store windows surrounding the plaza were brimming with Christmas gifts, all designed to kick off the holiday season. And if window displays alone weren't enough to bring out the Christmas spirit, in the center of the plaza stood the mammoth Gotham Plaza Christmas tree. A large crowd gathered around it, waiting for something to happen. As the sky grew dark, a woman's voice could be heard.

"It's time for tonight's lighting of the tree!" the voice said happily. "How about that!"

A woman dressed in a snow bunny costume emerged from a platform near the tree. She wore a tiara and a banner over her chest that read "Ice Princess." Waving to the crowd, she scurried across the platform to a huge multicolored button. Using both hands, she pressed it — and the Gotham City Christmas tree lit up.

The crowd oohed and ahhed with pleasure. The lighting of the tree was a grand Gotham City tradition. Thousands attended the event every holiday season. And this year was no exception. Everyone loved seeing the tree come alive in a blast of cheery colors.

Off to the side of the plaza, watching through a barred sewer grate, was a pair of familiar beady eyes. Older now, but no less frightening, the eyes narrowed to tiny slits in the darkness. A pair of black webbed hands curled around the bars and gripped them tightly, as a strange cackling voice floated in the air.

"I know when you are sleeping, I know when you're awake . . ."

Alfred Pennyworth, Bruce Wayne's butler and friend, rushed along the crowded street toward yet another jammed department store. Christmas shopping for Master Bruce was such a drain, he thought. As he passed by the sewer grating, he could have sworn he heard someone singing. But before he could take a look, a paperboy grabbed his attention.

"Read about the latest sighting of the penguin creature!" the kid shouted, pressing the paper toward Alfred. "Missing link between man and bird!"

Alfred eyed the newspaper headline. "PENGUIN: MAN OR MYTH OR SOMETHING WORSE?" it declared in black and white. Alfred shook his head. Ridiculous! Reading such piffle was such a waste of time.

Then Alfred suddenly remembered the singing in the sewer. Could it be —? He turned to look back at the grating, and just as he did, the pair of slimy flippers disappeared back into the darkness. It happened so fast it must have been Alfred's imagination.

High above the Gotham Plaza crowd, in the executive offices of Shreck's Department Store, two men looked down on the city — their city. Max Shreck, owner of the store and one of Gotham City's richest citizens, smiled at his personal friend the Mayor. The Mayor pointed out the Christmas tree in the plaza below and smiled. "Well, here's hoping Gotham just might have its first merry Christmas in a good long while," he said.

Shreck nodded. But there was something else on his mind. Right now seemed as good a time as any to bring it up. "I feel almost vulgar, in this Yuletide context," he said, "about mentioning the new power plant. But if we're gonna break ground, I'll need permits, tax incentives . . . that sort of pesky nonsense."

The Mayor looked at Shreck with genuine surprise. What was all this about power plants? Gotham City didn't need any more power plants! The city had enough energy to last till the next century!

Shreck had anticipated this reaction. He moved close to the Mayor, patted him on the back, and smiled. "I'm planning ahead for a revitalized Gotham City, so we can light the whole plaza without worrying about brownouts!" Shreck eyed the Mayor suspiciously. "Do you like the sound of 'brownouts?' " he asked, as the Mayor shuddered. "Do you?" he pressed. "Well?"

Before the Mayor could answer, Shreck's office door opened to admit his son, Chip, and his secretary, Selina Kyle. Chip, a big, blond twenty-two-year-old, looked like the typical, All-American football hero hunk. Selina was the type of woman who could have been quite a beauty if only she'd change her old-fashioned hairstyle and get

7

rid of her old-fashioned glasses. Right now, she was playing the perfect secretary, carrying a tray of coffee for her boss and his guest.

Time for me to wrap this up, Shreck thought. He curved his arm over the Mayor's shoulder and pulled him close, while gesturing out to the city beyond the window. "Imagine a Gotham City of the future," he said, "lit up like a blanket of stars . . . but blinking on and off, embarrassingly low on juice. Frankly, I cringe, Mr. Mayor." Shreck wanted a moment to let this horrifying prospect sink in, but it was not to be.

"Dad . . . Mr. Mayor," Chip interrupted, pointing to the clock on the wall. "It's time to go downstairs and bring joy to the masses."

The Mayor nodded to Chip, then turned toward Shreck. "Sorry," he said, all business once again. "You'll have to submit reports, blueprints, and plans through the usual channels."

Shreck could feel his temper rise. That wasn't what he wanted to hear. The time had come for him to play hardball with the Mayor . . . maybe then he could see his way to help Shreck's plan succeed. But before Shreck could utter a word, Selina beat him to the punch. "Um, I have a suggestion," she said, placing the coffee tray down on Shreck's huge circular conference table. "Well, really more of just a question —"

Shreck turned toward Selina angrily, shooting her a silencing glare. "I'm afraid we haven't properly housebroken Ms. Kyle," he apologized to the Mayor. "In the plus column, though, she brews one heckuva cup of coffee." As Shreck laughed heartily, he edged the Mayor toward the door. Best to continue this discussion elsewhere, he thought, away from Selina's foolish interruptions. A moment later, all three were gone, leaving Selina alone in the office with her fresh, bubbling coffee.

"Corn dog!" Selina cursed herself. How could she be so stupid? What had she done? Here she was, administrative assistant to one of Gotham City's top executives, and every time she opened her mouth, all she could do was make a fool of herself! "Actually, more of a question," she mimicked herself. She'd never prove she has a brain this way. "You stupid corn dog!" she muttered, slapping herself in the head. "Corn dog." Slap. "Corn dog." Slap. "CORN DOG!"

Two hundred feet below, Shreck and the Mayor, accompanied by Chip, made their way from the huge, happy cat's-head-shaped clock that hung over the doors of Shreck's Department Store toward a stage in the center of Gotham Plaza. Along the way, they were mobbed by citizens and press photographers, all anxious to get a glimpse of Gotham City's most famous citizens. Shreck and the Mayor moved slowly through the crowd, shaking hands and smiling as the flashbulbs popped around them, preserving each moment for tomorrow's newspapers.

Once on the stage, Shreck decided it was time to continue the conversation left unfinished in his office.

Now, while all of Gotham City watched and applauded, he'd move in for the kill.

"I have enough signatures," he whispered through clenched, smiling teeth, "from Shreck employees alone, to warrant a recall. That's not a threat. Just simple math."

The Mayor's Adam's apple jumped in his throat as he gulped, but his smile never faded. "Maybe," he said, refusing to be bullied, even by Gotham City's most important businessman. "But you don't have an issue, Max. Nor do you have a candidate." The Mayor motioned for the crowd to quiet down. Then he stepped up to the microphone. "The man who's given this city so much is here," he proclaimed, "to keep giving. Welcome Gotham's own Santa Claus, Max Shreck."

As she sat at her desk outside Shreck's office, Selina Kyle could swear she heard the thunderous applause for her boss coming up from the street below. But she was too busy jotting down a note to get up and take a look out the window. The note she wrote simply said "Obey," and she added it to the others sticking to the side of her computer. Notes with messages like "Don't 'get' jokes," and "Save it for your diary." Her eyes lingered sadly on all these messages to herself a moment, until the telephone rang. She looked toward the phone, but her eyes stopped dead when they glanced over a legal pad. On it was scrawled a single word: "Speech."

"Darn," Selina muttered as she grabbed her boss's speech and bolted toward the door. "DARN!"

On the stage in the center of Gotham Plaza, Max Shreck had a similar reaction as he stepped to the podium. "Forgot ... my ... speech," he whispered to Chip through clenched teeth. "Remind me to take it out on Selina." Then he turned to the microphone. Without a prepared speech, he'd have to improvise. "In this season of our savior's birth," he began, "I wish I could hand out world peace and unconditional love, wrapped in a big bow."

The crowd expressed its appreciation with a roar of delight. He looked down on them affectionately, as if they were his subjects. Then he noticed *they* were not looking at *him:* instead, their attention was directed at something being driven onto the street just above the plaza. Shreck gazed over to see what it was, and his mouth dropped open in awe. A gargantuan Christmas present wrapped in red paper with a colossal green bow! It must have been bigger than a truck! The Mayor stepped up to Shreck. "Great idea," he said with true admiration.

"But not mine," Shreck answered, puzzled.

The entire crowd watched as the package came to a halt. All were curious about what would happen next, but none more than Police Commissioner James Gordon, who tensely watched the scene unfold. This wasn't in the program for tonight, Gordon thought. He was here to

11

help control the crowds that always gathered on the night of the lighting of the Christmas tree. Usually there was *some* trouble, but never anything more serious than a couple of pickpockets or a gang of drunken rowdies.

This was different. He felt that in his gut. From a distance, he peered at the box, and could make out wheels churning and feet moving under the bottom edge. He squinted to get a better look —

And three motorcycles burst through the side of the box, engines roaring as they leaped into the crowd. The drivers wore huge death's-head masks. So amusing under normal circumstances — but right now, so deadly! Even as the three cycles tore into the crowd, a fourth broke through the side of the box, jumped over a railing, and landed right in the middle of the plaza, in front of the tree. A fifth cycle emerged, following the first three, to chase down a group of Christmas carolers. In a split second, the five singers had been hurled to the ground.

But the box still held a few more surprises. Suddenly, the top of the box exploded, and, in a sea of confetti, five acrobats were launched into the crowd. They flipped, cartwheeled, spun, and leaped all over the plaza, knocking down pedestrians and police, smashing anything that stood between them and their destination.

And to Commissioner Gordon, who stood watching helplessly, it seemed their destination was the world-famous Christmas tree. As the crowd surged away from the plaza in terror, Gordon realized he was in over his head. He turned angrily to one of his officers. "What are you waiting for?" he barked. "The signal!"

Moments later, a shard of light broke through the fog-filled Gotham City night, tearing across the sky for all to see, a silhouette of a bat at its apex. And although the sight of the familiar symbol reassured everyone who saw it, the Bat-Signal was lit to capture the attention of one man.

Millionaire Bruce Wayne sat in darkness. He usually felt most comfortable that way. It helped him think, and thinking helped him pass the time while he waited for the call to action. He thought about his parents now and then. And about the night his life was changed forever. He remembered the gunman who killed them both, and his tearful vow of revenge. How he'd get the murderer and all the others like him. He ached for — *lived* for — the opportunity. And as the reflection of the Bat-Signal appeared on his living room wall, Bruce Wayne knew he would get it once again.

From his perch below the streets of Gotham Plaza, he could see it all. He flapped his flippers merrily as he watched through the sewer grating, his beady eyes aglow with the blazing lights of carnage in the streets. The cyclists and acrobats were only the beginning. He'd pulled out all the stops for this little spectacle.

At one end of the plaza, the Fire Breather had smashed though one of the toy store display windows and bellowed a ball of flame onto all the toys, burning them to a crisp.

On the stage, the Organ Grinder turned the crank of his innocent-looking organ box toward the Christmas tree. Instead of music, bullets spewed out, blasting the tree ornaments to bits as his monkey chattered gleefully. Nearby, the Fat Clown, the Sword Swallower, the Knife Thrower, and the Poodle Lady stormed the stage and headed toward Shreck, the Mayor, and Chip. Of the three, only the Mayor had the courage to step forward.

"What do you want from me?" he asked.

"Not you," the Sword Swallower answered, laughing. "Shreck." As he moved toward Shreck, Chip rose and blocked the way.

"You'll have to go through me," he said defiantly.

The Fat Clown nearby laughed mockingly. "All this courage," he smirked. "Goosebump City."

Chip stood his ground — but when the Knife Thrower tossed a knife to nick Chip's ear, and the Sword Swallower pulled a sword out of his mouth and pressed it against Chip's neck, he panicked. "Dad!" he cried. "Save yourself!" And as Max Shreck leaped from the stage and fled into the crowd, Chip knew his father was doing just that.

All this the creature below the streets could see from the sewer grating. Each passing moment of havoc brought more gleeful joy to his beady eyes. But the main event was yet to come. And as the Batmobile screeched onto the plaza, the creature knew it was about to start.

Inside the Batmobile, Batman attempted to assess the situation. To the left, a trio of Stilt Walkers viciously kicked members of the crowd. Nearby, a group of circus-style gangsters and bikers were randomly selecting citizens to beat. Easy enough to deal with, Batman thought. As the Batmobile passed by the Stilt Walkers, twin blades sprouted from the its sides, slicing the stilts in half and toppling the Stilt Walkers.

The Batmobile then turned to face the gangsters and bikers. Black metal Batdiscs shot out of the car's sides, instantly taking out four of them. As the remainder fled, three clowns began firing machine guns at the oncoming Batmobile. One of the clowns dived out of the way as the car sped past, but the other two leaped atop the Batmobile's hood. They continued firing into the Batmobile's bulletproof windshield as it sped toward the end of the plaza. There, the Fire Breather was still at work turning the remainder of the toys into black ash.

Hearing the roar of the engine behind him, the Fire Breather turned from the storefront as the Batmobile sped directly toward him. He's not gonna stop, the Fire Breather thought — just as Batman jammed on the brakes. The Batmobile came to a halt mere inches away from the Fire Breather, but the clown riders on the hood were ripped loose by the sudden stop and were launched onto the pavement.

Not doing too badly here, Batman thought. He

15

remembered he still had one clown to take care of, the one who had ducked out of the way of the Batmobile. He twisted a square black knob on the console to activate the hydraulic lift. Instantly, a powerful steel jack bolted from the Batmobile's undercarriage, lifting the entire car up and turning it around to face the fleeing clown. Another turn of the knob, and the jack slammed back inside the car.

Batman was about to take off when he glanced into his rearview mirror to see the Fire Breather stagger up behind him. The Fire Breather inhaled deeply — and Batman gunned the engine. Before the Fire Breather could exhale, he was wrapped in the Batmobile's exhaust flames.

The Terrifying Clown looked desperate as the Batmobile bore down on him. His luck had run out, he figured. Now there was only one thing left to do — grab the nearest innocent bystander and use her to make an escape. He glanced to his left, and noticed a woman with an old-fashioned haircut and old-fashioned glasses. She was just standing there, scanning the crowd as if looking for someone. She clutched a few sheets of paper in her hand. She's the one, the Terrifying Clown thought.

Selina couldn't figure it out. When she'd left the office, Shreck's speech in her hand, everything down below seemed so normal. Now it was just craziness down here. Where had Shreck gone? And what about Chip? She wondered whether it really mattered. After forgetting to give Shreck his speech, she doubted she had a job anymore. Still, she should at least *try* to find her soon-to-be-ex-boss . . .

Just then the Terrifying Clown grabbed her and pressed a stun gun to her neck. He turned her around on the heel of her shoe, which broke off just as the Batmobile skidded to a stop in front of them.

Selina looked at the Batmobile, then down at the heel of her shoe. "I probably shouldn't mention this," she said, "but this is a very serious pair of shoes you just ruined."

The clown couldn't believe it. I've got a stun gun glued to her neck, and *she's* worried about her shoes! As he considered letting this hostage go and trying to grab a more cooperative one, the Batmobile's door whooshed open and Batman emerged. The clown stiffened. This nutty woman would have to do.

"Listen up, Mister Man-bat," The Terrifying Clown snarled "You take one step closer and I'll —" In response, Batman stopped, whipped out his grappling gun, and fired a spear toward the clown — a spear that missed the target and slammed deep into the wall behind the clown.

The Terrifying Clown chuckled. Some shot, he thought, as Batman pulled sharply on the wire connected to the spear. The spear came loose, pulling with it a chunk of the wall, which smacked the clown in the back of his head. Dazed, the clown staggered about, turning to face Selina. "You shouldn't have left the other heel," she sneered, delivering a stunning kick to the Terrifying Clown's face

17

that sent him crashing to the ground. Not bad, Selina thought, impressed by her work. All those years of martial arts training had finally paid off. But would that be enough to impress . . . *him?*

Selina watched as Batman approached. He seemed so . . . good-looking, even with that strange black mask and cape. There was something oh-so-mysterious about him. As he leaned over to examine the unconscious clown, Selina tried to think of some way to introduce herself. As his finger brushed over the strange red triangle tattoo over the clown's eye, she wondered if he was married or single. And as he turned and raced off with barely a "gotta go," she wondered why all the men in her life always did that.

At that moment, in one of Gotham Plaza's many tiny alleyways, Max Shreck was about to make his triumphant return. He'd seen it all from his hiding place: the attack, Batman's appearance, the battle — and now he was certain it was safe to rejoin the crowd. He smiled to himself, adjusted his tie, and mopped a bit of the sweat from his brow. Just then, the grating Shreck was standing on cracked in half, sucking him into the darkness. As soon as he was gone, the grating popped back into position, as if Shreck had never been there at all.

What a day, Selina thought as she entered her apartment. "Honey, I'm home," she proclaimed, then laughed to herself. "Oh, I forgot. I'm not married."

Some joke, she said to herself. There was no one else in the Kyle household — at least no one human. She took off her coat and hung it on its proper hook, then walked across her pink carpet, past her fully stocked doll house, her stuffed animal collection, and the big happy neon sign that proclaimed "Hello there!" to a world that never looked, to the half-open window. A beautiful cat sat just outside, as if awaiting her arrival. "Miss Kitty!" Selina said, smiling. "Back from more escapades?"

In response, Miss Kitty hopped back inside, purring contentedly as Selina stroked her fluffy coat. "What did you just purr?" Selina asked. " 'How can you be so pathetic?' Yes," she added defensively, "to you I may seem pathetic. But I'm a working girl. Gotta pay the rent." Still, she had to admit, her life *was* pretty boring and sad. As if to prove the point, she walked over to the answering machine. Four messages.

The first was from her mother, begging her to leave Gotham City and come back home to live. Typical. The second was from her poor excuse for a boyfriend, canceling a trip they'd planned together. Expected. The third was from a self-defense class she'd joined, complaining she'd missed a recent meeting. What else was new? The fourth sounded vaguely familiar, until she realized it was her own voice coming from the machine.

"Hi, Selina," the message began. "This is yourself calling. To remind you that you'll have to come all the way

19

back to the office unless you remembered to bring home the Bruce Wayne file, because the meeting's on Wednesday and Max Slavemaster wants every pertinent fact at your lovely tapered fingertips!"

Oh, no! She'd completely forgotten! She slapped herself on the head, hard. "You stupid corn dog!" she muttered as she grabbed her coat and fled the apartment. "Corn dog! Deep-fried! Corn dog!"

The last thing Max Shreck remembered, he was preparing to step out of an alleyway after Batman had taken care of those criminal circus performers. He remembered falling — and that was about all.

Now he was sitting tied up in a chair! He glanced to the side, and there, mere inches from his face, was a penguin! Shreck yelped with fright. The penguin yelped back. What the heck is going on here? Shreck wondered. He looked around, to discover that he and the penguin weren't alone.

He was surrounded by the Red Triangle Circus Gang. They were all there, fresh from their battle with Batman. The Poodle Lady. The Organ Grinder and his monkeys. The clowns. The Sword Swallower. The Stilt Walkers. Somehow, they had all managed to escape, and Shreck couldn't begin to imagine what they planned to do to him now. He screamed in terror. As one, the entire gang burst out laughing.

Over the sound of the laughter Shreck heard the hum of an electric generator. It must be some kind of air-conditioning unit, he reasoned, since the underground cavern seemed to be growing colder by the minute. From the corner of his eye he noticed more penguins — hundreds of them, in all shapes and sizes, standing near the generator. The largest of them — if Shreck could believe his eyes — was actually wearing a grimy coat and holding an open umbrella over his head!

Even though he was frightened and freezing, Shreck almost laughed at the sight. An umbrella! he thought, as the clownish creature moved closer. They can teach those birds to do anything! The big bird waddled close to Shreck and closed the umbrella to reveal his face.

It wasn't a penguin at all. It was THE Penguin. The creature all the newspapers were talking about. The Bird-man that lurked below the city streets. With a nose that looked like a beak, and hands that looked like flippers. He was horrifying. Shreck opened his mouth to scream but nothing came out.

"I believe the word you're looking for," The Penguin quipped as he toyed with his umbrella, "is 'A-A-A-A-A-GH!!' " A sudden flash of fire burst from the umbrella's tip.

"My God," Shreck groaned. "Please — don't hurt me —"

The Penguin placed the umbrella aside and smiled. Hurt him? No way. He had something else in mind. "Odd

21

as it may seem, Max," he said, "we have something in common. We're both perceived as monsters. But somehow, you're a well-respected monster, and I am . . . to date . . . *not*." He picked up another nearby umbrella to try it out. This one shot knives.

Shreck gulped, but tried to be brave. "Frankly, I feel that's a bum rap," he said. "I'm a businessman. Tough, yes. Shrewd, okay. But that doesn't make me a monster —"

"Don't embarrass yourself, Max," The Penguin interrupted as he revealed yet another umbrella, this one with a swirling, hypnotic design printed on its fabric. "I know all about you. What you hide, I discover. Get the picture?"

Helpless to do anything else, Shreck nodded that he did. The Penguin smiled. Good. Now he could get to the point of this little meeting. "I've been lingering down here too long," he said with a touch of sadness. "It's high time for me to reemerge. With your help. I wasn't born in the sewer. I come from —" he pointed toward the streets up above — "like you. And, like you, I want some respect . . . a recognition of my basic humanity. But most of all, I want to find out who I am. By finding my parents. Learning my 'human' name. Simple stuff that the good people of Gotham take for granted."

I get it now, Shreck thought. The little freak wants me to help him. Just one more charity case looking for a handout. Well, Shreck wasn't having any of it. He puffed out his chest boldly. "And exactly *why* am I gonna help *you*?"

"Well," The Penguin said, as if expecting this response, "let's start with a batch of toxic waste from your 'clean' textile plant. There's a whole lagoon of this crud in the back."

Shreck shook his head, unconvinced. "Yawn. That coulda come from anyplace."

"What about the documents that prove you own half the firetraps in Gotham?"

Uh-oh, Shreck thought. He's getting close — but not close enough to hurt. "If there *were* such documents," he said in his best public relations voice, "I would have seen to it that they were shredded."

The Penguin held out his flipper, and one of the clowns handed him a pile of taped-up documents. Shreck groaned.

"A lot of tape and a little patience make all the difference," The Penguin grinned. And before he forgot, there was one more card he wanted to play. His beady eyes peered closely at Shreck. He wanted to savor the businessman's reaction. "By the way," he finally asked, "how's Fred Adkins, your old partner?"

That did it. Shreck was totally rattled now. "Fred. Fred?" he stammered. "He's . . . actually, he's been on an extended vacation and —"

From under his coat, The Penguin pulled out a discolored human hand and waved it happily toward

23

Shreck. "Hi, Max," he mumbled, trying not to move his lips, "Remember me? I'm Fred's hand!" Then, dropping the ventriloquist act, he continued. "Want to greet any other body parts? Remember, Max, you flush it, I flaunt it."

Shreck breathed in deeply. It was hopeless. The Penguin had enough evidence on Shreck's illegal activities to send him away for life. Shreck was beaten — but he slowly managed a smile.

"You know what, Mr. Penguin, sir," he said humbly, "I think I could perhaps orchestrate a little welcome-home scenario for you . . ."

The Penguin smiled. Now *that* was more like it.

As the leading public official in Gotham City, it was the Mayor's duty to tour any local disaster area. The morning after the criminal circus's attack, Gotham Plaza certainly fit the part. For the occasion, the Mayor was accompanied by his wife, their newborn child, and a solemn Max Shreck. Reporters with video cameras followed their every step as they walked past the burned-out automobiles, shattered windows, and smashed Christmas tree ornaments that littered the streets. The more he saw, the more outraged the Mayor became. Finally, he turned to the waiting cameras.

"I tell you this, not just as an official, but as a husband

and father," he said, "last night's eruption of lawlessness will never happ —"

An acrobat flipped up over the remains of the Christmas tree, landing mere inches from the Mayor's wife. He stepped toward the stunned woman and gracefully snatched the child from her arms. The Mayor turned and lunged toward the kidnapper — and received a kick in the chest for his trouble.

With astonishing speed, the acrobat zipped through the shocked crowd. He was already as good as gone —

Until he fell into an open manhole. The crowd rushed up to surround the hole. They looked down into the silent darkness. A moment, and Shreck had pushed his way to the front of the crowd. He stared down into it, as if waiting for something to happen.

"NOOO!" someone screamed from deep inside the manhole. "Get away! Get —" Sounds of violent struggle followed, and then the terrified acrobat scrambled back out the manhole and ran off through the crowd. No one tried to stop him. The eyes of the entire crowd were glued on what next emerged from the hole.

The Mayor's baby! As if by magic, the child seemed to float in the air above the hole. Then the crowd noticed an arm with a strange birdlike flipper holding the baby up. And as the baby rose higher and higher, the crowd could see a strange birdlike head. And an even stranger birdlike body. The crowd gasped. It was The Penguin creature all of Gotham City had heard about, but none had ever really seen. It was incredible! Almost as incredible as the strange duck-shaped vehicle that lifted The Penguin and the child out of the manhole and onto the pavement.

The television cameras began to roll, instantly transmitting the scene before them into the homes of millions of Gothamites. "This morning's miracle, Gotham will never forget," the TV reporter announced as the Mayor's wife snatched her baby out of The Penguin's deformed hands, and hugged The Penguin. He smiled sheepishly, almost embarrassed at this public display of affection. "Until today, he'd been another tabloid myth," the reporter continued, "but now this bashful man-beast can proudly take his place alongside our own legendary Batman."

As the cameras continued filming the historic moment, Max Shreck squeezed through the crowd and placed his arm around The Penguin's shoulder. He whispered something into The Penguin's ear, and The Penguin took a meek little bow before the cameras.

A reporter asked The Penguin what kind of reward he'd want for saving the Mayor's child. The Penguin thought about it for a moment and then, with tear-filled eyes, looked directly at the camera. "All I want in return," he choked, "is the chance to find my folks . . . and thus find out who I am . . . and then, just try . . . to understand why . . . they did what I guess they felt they had to do, to a child who was born a little . . . different. A child who spent his first Christmas, and many since, in a sewer . . ." The Penguin turned away, unable to continue.

Miles away, in the elegant living room of Wayne Manor, Bruce Wayne watched The Penguin's speech and sympathized. Living without parents was a tragedy he understood only too well.

"Mr. Wayne," Alfred suddenly asked. "Something wrong?"

"No, nothing," Bruce murmured. "Ah . . . his parents . . . I . . ." He lowered his head sadly. "I hope he finds them."

Over the next few days, Gotham City's newest hero began the quest to find his parents. In the Gotham City Hall of Records, The Penguin sat surrounded by hundreds of thousands of file folders marked "Birth Certificates." He patiently examined each and every one, and from time to time jotted down a name. Soon, he had a tall stack of notebooks filled with them.

The streets were dark and empty as the Batmobile cruised through downtown Gotham City. It was quiet, almost too quiet. As Batman scanned the streets from inside the Batmobile, Alfred's image appeared on the dashboard's video screen.

"The city's been noticeably quiet since the thwarted baby-napping," he said, "yet still you patrol. What about eating? Sleeping? You won't be much good to anyone else if you don't look after yourself."

But Batman knew what he was looking for — he just hadn't found it yet. "The Red Triangle Circus Gang," he said. "They're jackals, Alfred. They hunt in packs, at night." If, after the attack on Gotham Plaza they had decided to lie low, it must have been for a reason. In his bones, Batman could feel they were planning something big. If only he could figure out what it was.

As the Batmobile passed by the Hall of Records, Alfred had one more question. "Are you concerned about that strange, heroic Penguin person?"

Batman looked up at the records building. A single lit window there indicated The Penguin was still at work inside. "Funny you should ask, Alfred," he finally said as he drove past. "Maybe I *am* a bit concerned."

The next day, all of Gotham City was abuzz with the news. The Penguin had done it. After hours of research, he'd finally found his parents. Now he was going to meet them. The press, accompanied by a huge crowd of curiosity seekers, gathered at the gates of Gotham City Cemetery to witness the occasion. The police were out in force too, erecting barricades to prevent the onlookers from getting too close. After all, this was a very important moment for The Penguin. He deserved a little privacy.

The crowd watched as The Penguin knelt before a pair of gravestones. Chiseled onto the cool gray marble were the names Tucker Cobblepot and Esther Cobblepot.

Video cameras began to whir, recording the touching event for home audiences. The Penguin produced a pair of wilted roses from inside his sleeve and placed them on the graves. After a moment of silence, he rose and, with tears welling up in his beady little eyes, walked back to the cemetery gates and the crowd waiting for him there.

"So, Mr. Penguin —" a reporter began, but was cut short by The Penguin's indignant glare.

"A 'penguin' is a bird that cannot fly," he declared. "I am a man. I have a name. It's Oswald Cobblepot."

"Mr. Cobblepot!" the reporter continued. "You'll never get a chance to settle up with 'em, right?"

"It's human nature to fear the unusual," The Penguin answered after thinking a moment. "Perhaps when I held my Tiffany baby rattle with a shiny flipper, and not five chubby digits, they freaked." Then he looked at the crowd, whose eyes sparkled with tears of sympathy. "But I forgive them."

The crowd cheered. The Penguin was their hero of the hour.

He had them right where he wanted them.

By the time the evening papers hit the stands, all of Gotham City was talking about The Penguin. "PENGUIN FORGIVES PARENTS," the headline read. "I'M FULLY AT PEACE WITH MYSELF AND THE WORLD." The public seemed so touched by this tragic figure, they could speak of little else. His every word was embraced by the city; his every sentence proved their passion for him was well deserved. "My heart is filled with love," read one quote. "I feel five feet tall." This creature, who was once feared as something less than human, was now suddenly much, much more. So noble, so dignified, he was an example for others to follow. In this Christmas season, The Penguin was a true leader of men.

And while all of Gotham City read the evening paper's Penguin stories, down in the Batcave under Wayne Manor Bruce Wayne was reading a newspaper too. Only this newspaper was on microfiche, and it had first appeared many years before. Bruce was attempting to trace the origins of the mysterious Red Triangle Circus, and the newspaper article on the screen before him was the first of many dealing with the subject.

The sequence of stories began innocently. "The Red Triangle Circus put on a swell show last night, with fierce lions," the first article read. Bruce skipped ahead to an article that appeared a few years later: "Red Triangle Circus has returned for a two-week stay. Kids will love . . ." Still, there was nothing to indicate why the traveling troop had turned from wholesome entertainment to criminal activities.

The third article contained something that might have been a clue. "The Red Triangle Circus is back," it reported, "with a freak show that may not be suitable for your kids, featuring a bearded lady, the world's fattest man, and an aquatic bird-boy . . ." As Bruce stared at the screen, Alfred entered the Batcave. He looked at Bruce, then read the passage on the screen.

"Why are you now determined to prove that this Penguin — er, Mr. Cobblepot — is not what he seems?" Alfred asked after completing the article. "Must *you* be the only 'lonely man-beast' in town?"

In response, Bruce pressed a button to reveal a final newspaper article, this one from only a few years before. "After numerous reports of missing children in several towns," the article said, "police have closed down the Red Triangle's fairgrounds. However, at least one freak-show performer vanished before he could be questioned . . ."

Bruce turned to see if the butler saw the connection between The Penguin and the criminal circus. Alfred nodded sadly that he did. "I suppose you feel better now, sir," he said.

"No," Bruce answered solemnly. "Actually, I feel worse."

By two in the morning, Selina Kyle knew she was in trouble. There was no way she could organize all the material on her office desk for Shreck's meeting with Bruce Wayne tomorrow. Still, she had to give it her best shot. Her only alternative was unemployment. So she continued to scribble notes frantically onto her notepad — until she felt a hand on her shoulder. Spinning around, she came face-to-face with Max Shreck.

"Working late?" Shreck smiled. "I'm touched."

Selina cleared her throat, not wanting to let on she'd been scared half to death by Shreck's unexpected arrival. "I pulled all the files on the proposed power plant, and Mr. Wayne's hoped-for investment," she said, as she composed herself. "I've studied up on all of it. I even opened the protected files and —"

Shreck raised an eyebrow, curious. "And how did you open the protected files, may I ask?"

Selina beamed at her own industriousness. "Well, I figured that your password was 'Finster.' Your Chihuahua. And it was." Shreck nodded encouragingly for her to continue. "It's all very interesting," she said excitedly, "I mean, about how the power plant is a power plant in name only, since instead of generating power it'll sort of be" — she checked her notes to make sure she got this part right — "*sucking* power from Gotham City and stockpiling it. Which," she proudly concluded, "is a very novel approach, I'd say."

Selina's smile began to fade, however, when her boss calmly lit a match and set fire to her notepad. Suddenly, she suspected she'd done her research a little *too* well. Shreck smiled, but the strange gleam in his eye made Selina more nervous. She rose from her seat and backed away from her boss, who moved closer to her. "It's our secret, honest," she pleaded. "How can you be so mean to someone so meaningless?"

Shreck felt compelled to answer his secretary's question,

the way an executioner will honor a condemned man's final request. "The power plant is to be my pyramid," he said, as he cornered Selina against the window behind her desk. "My cathedral, my legacy to Chip. Nothing must prevent that."

Her back to the window, Selina had no place to turn. In an instant, Shreck was upon her, grabbing her tightly by the shoulders. Through tears of fear, Selina tried to act brave. "Okay, go ahead," she said defiantly. "Intimidate me, bully me, if it makes you feel big. I mean, it's not like you can just kill me —"

Shreck smiled sadly. "Actually," he said, "it's a lot like that."

And then he pushed her through the window.

Through the darkness, through the swirling snow, accompanied by fragments of window glass, Selina Kyle fell. Faster and faster — until she heard the sound of ripping canvas. Was that an awning she'd just fallen through? Did it matter? After all, she was falling too fast for a simple fabric awning to save her. But then she hit a second awning. And a third. And a fourth. And although she was still falling, her descent had slowed down enough for her to see that her final destination was a fluffy white snowdrift that had gathered in a dingy alleyway next to Shreck's Department Store.

She hit the snow with a force that knocked the wind out

33

of her. Had she survived? Had she broken any bones? She didn't know. She was certain only that she'd landed — but the world around her was still spinning out of control, and growing darker every moment. "Help me," she whimpered. "Someone . . ."

Shreck looked out his shattered window toward the street, but he didn't have to see his secretary's lifeless body to know what he'd done to her. He shook his head, unable to believe his own capacity for violence. He always believed he'd never let anything or anyone stand in the way of his business plans, but murder was a bit much. Still, he reasoned, what's done is done, and since he wasn't about to give himself up and go to prison, he had to think up a good story to cover Ms. Kyle's death.

As he pondered the possibilities, he turned from the window. His son, Chip, was standing in the doorway. Did he know? Had he seen it all? Better to assume he hadn't, and come up with an excuse right now. "It was terrible," Shreck began. "I leaned over, and accidentally knocked her out —"

Chip remained cool and collected as he shook his head. He had a better idea. "She jumped," he offered. "She'd been depressed."

Shreck stared at his son. Sonuvagun, he thought. The kid's a chip off the old block! "Yes, yes," Shreck said, smiling. Suicide was a *much* better reason. As Chip turned to leave the office, Shreck watched him with admiration. That's my boy, he thought.

Lying in the darkness, Selina felt a rhythmic pressure on her chest that seemed familiar and comforting. She felt her lips being parted, and air being pushed down her throat in short little bursts. In her half-conscious state she reasoned that a paramedic was performing life-giving C.P.R. on her; the thing was, she wasn't so sure she even wanted to live anymore. Look what life had done for her so far; she had no friends, no lovers, and her boss had just tried to kill her. She was completely alone. Maybe she was better off dead.

Then she heard the purring of cats. First one, then dozens, maybe hundreds of them. She felt them rubbing against her body, against her face, crawling over and around her. Lazily, she half-opened her eyes and saw Miss Kitty kneading her chest and breathing into her mouth. She smiled. She *did* have one friend. Miss Kitty. And Miss Kitty had brought all *her* friends to help Selina.

A Siamese whispered in her ear. A group of tabbies snuggled against her feet. An old tomcat bit her finger.

"OW!" Selina cried as her eyes flew open. She looked around. It wasn't her imagination — she *was* surrounded by hundreds of cats. Of all the creatures on earth, only they wanted to help her. Only they offered her unconditional love. Only they were her friends.

And in that moment Selina Kyle made a decision. She would become one of them.

Although bruised and bloody, Selina paid little attention to her injuries as she staggered into her quaint, comfortable apartment an hour later. If she was going to become a cat, she had changes to make here.

With cans of black spray paint in each hand, she set about redecorating her apartment, attacking everything pink and eggshell. In moments, her carpet, couch, and walls bore dripping black streaks.

Panting heavily, she looked at all the relics of her lost childhood; the stuffed animals, the doll house, the photographs. It all seemed so alien to her now. She smashed the house to pieces, tore the animals to shreds, and stuffed whatever was left into the garbage.

She curled up in a corner, catching her breath. Still, something gnawed at her. Something was missing. She found some pieces of leather, and with a needle began stitching the pieces together into a costume. Soon it was complete.

She put the costume on. It felt good. Stretchy. Slinky. Sinful. Just like a cat.

As the sun rose over the city the next morning, Bruce Wayne walked through the remains of Gotham Plaza.

Around him, mechanics still attempted to restore the tree to its former glory. But Bruce knew it was hopeless. Christmas in Gotham City had been ruined. And he was determined to find the people responsible.

But right now he had other things to do. He entered the Shreck building and rode the elevator up to Max Shreck's office. As he entered, Shreck and his son were staring out a shattered glass picture window.

"Hmm," Bruce murmured. "Primitive ventilation."

Shreck turned, the worry on his face quickly replaced by anger and frustration. "Damn those carny bolsheviks the other night," he began. "Throwing bricks through my windows . . ."

Bruce looked at the floor. "No," he corrected. "No glass on the inside."

Shreck looked nervous. "Weird, huh?" he asked. Bruce thought about it as Chip led them into the conference room. Bruce took a seat, but Shreck continued to pace nervously.

"I'd offer you coffee," Shreck explained, "but my assistant is using her vacation time."

"Good time, too," Bruce answered. He watched Shreck closely. "Everyone but the bandits seem to be slacking off till after New Year's."

If Bruce was looking for a reaction, he certainly got it. Shreck sat down across the table from him. "Not sure I like the inference," he said. "I'm pushing this power plant now only because it'll cost more later."

Bruce opened his briefcase and laid a bound report on the conference table. "I commissioned this report," he said casually. "I thought you should see it." Shreck flipped through it and yawned. "Here's the point, Max," Bruce continued. "Gotham City has a power surplus. I'm sure you know that. So the question is: what's your angle?"

Shreck jumped to his feet. "A 'power surplus?' " he exclaimed. "Bruce, shame on you — no such thing! One can never have too much power!" Behind Shreck, Chip nodded in agreement. "If my life has any meaning," Shreck continued, "that's the meaning."

But Bruce had already made up his mind. "Max," he insisted, "I'm going to fight you on this. The Mayor and I have already spoken and we see eye-to-eye here. So —"

Shreck cut him off. "Mayors come and go," he said slyly. In the end, Shreck would win the fight. He always did.

But Bruce had a punch or two of his own. "Guess we'll find out, Max," he suggested as he shut his briefcase and rose. " 'Course, I don't have a crime boss like Cobblepot in my corner . . ."

Shreck faked outrage, but inside he was worried. Just how much did Wayne know and how did he know it? He quickly found out.

"Oswald controls the Red Triangle Circus Gang," Bruce declared. "I can't prove it, but we both know it's true."

Shreck's face reddened. "Wayne," he thundered, "I'll not stand for mudslinging in this office. If my assistant were here, she'd already have escorted you out, to —"

"Wherever he wants," a female voice interrupted.

All three turned to see Selina sashay into the room. "Preferably some nightspot, grotto, or hideaway," she continued, smiling at Bruce.

What a change, Bruce thought. He barely remembered her as the mousy woman he'd met as Batman a few nights before. Selina was now fashionably dressed, with a new modern hairstyle. But it was more than that. She seemed different now. More self-assured. Vibrant. Sexy.

To his horror, Shreck instantly recognized her as the woman he'd thrown from his window hours before. "Selina?" he mumbled, stunned. "Selina ... Selina ..." He couldn't believe she was still alive.

"That's my name, Maxamillions," Selina said, smiling confidently. "Don't wear it out, babe, or I'll make you buy me a new one."

Shreck laughed halfheartedly at the joke. He'd have to deal with this — later. Right now, however, introductions were in order. "Uh, Selina," he said, trying to get a grasp of the situation, "this is, uh, Bruce Wayne."

Bruce smiled and took her hand. He noticed the fresh bandage wrapped around it. "What happened?" he asked.

"Yes, did — did you injure yourself on that ski slope?" Shreck interrupted nervously. "Is that why you cut short your vacation and came back?"

Selina shrugged. "Maybe that broken window over there had something to do with it," she answered, getting a little pleasure from watching Shreck squirm, "or maybe not. It's blurry."

Shreck turned to Chip. Neither was certain if Selina had any memory of the previous night's events. They'd talk it over, after they got rid of Wayne. "Selina," Shreck asked, "Please show out Mr. Wayne."

Selina smiled at Bruce and motioned for him to follow. Why not, Bruce figured. He liked this woman, enough to want to get to know her better.

The instant both were gone, Shreck headed toward the phone. "You buy this 'blurry' business?" Chip asked.

"Women," Shreck answered as he dialed. "Nothing surprises me. Who even knew Selina had a brain to damage? Bottom line," he continued, "she tries to blackmail us, we drop her out a higher window. Meanwhile, I got badder fish to fry." On the other end of the line, someone picked up the phone. "Oswald, please," Shreck said.

The top floor of the abandoned two-story warehouse on Gotham City's north side was anything but empty. Thanks to Max Shreck's generosity, The Penguin and the Red Triangle Circus Gang had found a home, far from the prying eyes of Gotham City's reporters. A dozen of them roughhoused on the filthy loft floor. Every once in a while, another member of the troop would crawl in through the vent Shreck had provided to allow them to come and go in secrecy.

In a corner, sitting by an open window, The Penguin reviewed the names he'd gathered at the Hall of Records. Referring to the Gotham City White Pages every few moments, he'd scribble down addresses next to the names.

"For you, boss," the Organ Grinder said, holding a phone in his hand.

The Penguin snatched it with his flipper. "Yeah, what is it?" he barked. "I'm busy up here."

On the other end of the line, Shreck smiled. "Good," he answered. "Stay busy up there." He thought of the ground floor of the warehouse, and how, even as he spoke, volunteers were beginning to dress up the freshly painted storefront with posters and flags and banners. "I've got plans for us, Oswald," he said mysteriously.

But The Penguin was too busy working on his lists to care. "'Plans.'" he repeated. "Swell. Later." He slammed down the receiver. He had more important things to do.

It was time for a test run. Earlier that evening, she'd added a pair of accessories to her costume: ten razor-sharp metal talons, one for each dainty fingertip, and a menacing leather bullwhip. Now, Selina thought, Catwoman was ready to prowl.

From her fire-escape perch, she heard the plea for help from the alley below. "Help, Batman!" a woman cried, but there were no heroes to save her here. No, it was just she and the mugger now, who was busy rummaging through her purse. "Please don't hurt me," she begged. "I'll do anything —"

Suddenly, Catwoman leaped onto his back. "I just love a big strong man who's not afraid to show it with someone half his size," she purred.

The mugger scrambled free of Catwoman's deadly embrace, then turned and charged her.

She kicked him square in the head and went to work rearranging his face. A flurry of talons sent him squealing to the pavement in pain.

The woman rushed up to Catwoman's side. "Thank you, thank you," she cried. "I was so scared —" Without warning, Catwoman grabbed her and angrily pressed her against the alley wall.

"You make it so easy, don't you!" she hissed. "You pretty, pathetic young thing. Always waiting for some BatMAN to save you." Disgusted, she leaned toward the woman. "I'm CatWOMAN, hear me roar," she whispered into her ear.

Then she turned away, gaily cartwheeling out of the alley, and into the night.

"Close your eyes," Max Shreck insisted as he led The Penguin down the stairs to the storefront of his warehouse the next morning. Shreck knew The Penguin hated surprises, and was reluctant to leave his stupid lists and phonebooks even for a little while, but this part of Shreck's plan was too good to reveal without a little fanfare.

While the rest of the Red Triangle Circus Gang remained upstairs, Shreck led The Penguin into the middle of the room. "Ta-*da!*" he sang when The Penguin opened his eyes.

The storefront had been transformed overnight into the COBBLEPOT FOR MAYOR campaign headquarters. Balloons, posters, bunting, computers, and volunteers were everywhere. The volunteers cheered The Penguin's arrival. And much as he'd hate to admit it, The Penguin was struck speechless. Shreck held him close and tried to explain. "Someone's got to supplant our standing-in-the-way-of-progress mayor," he said, "and don't deny it, Mr. Cobblepot, your charisma is bigger than both of us."

The Penguin wasn't sure he heard right. "Mayor?" he asked.

"Mayor," Shreck affirmed.

But this didn't make any sense, The Penguin thought. Elections were held in November, and this was late December! "Elected officials can be recalled," Shreck pointed out. "Given the boot! Think of Nixon. Then think of you, Oswald Cobblepot, filling the void."

Yeah, The Penguin thought. Mayor Cobblepot. Had a nice ring to it. He liked it.

"We need signatures," Shreck continued. "To overturn the ballot. I can supply those. And we need one more thing. A catalyst. A trigger, an incident."

That part was easy, The Penguin thought. "You want

43

my old friends upstairs to drive the Mayor into a foaming frenzy?" he asked.

"Precisely," Shreck answered.

This could be good, The Penguin thought. Then he thought of something else. His lists. His brows furrowed at the thought of it. "I mustn't get sidetracked," he reminded himself. "I've got my own —" Agenda, he meant to say, but Shreck wasn't hearing any of it.

"Sidetracked?" Shreck interrupted. "Oswald, this is your chance to fulfill a destiny that your parents so carelessly discarded."

"Reclaim my birthright, y'mean?" The Penguin wondered. That was it exactly, Shreck insisted.

The Penguin mulled it over a bit. Sure, he could use the adulation of the masses. And it might be fun to get out every once in a while. Besides all that, think of the babes he'd get when he was the Mayor!

But what about his own plans? What about his revenge? He weighed his options a moment, before realizing that with a little luck, he could have it both ways. He turned to Shreck and the volunteers. "All right," he announced. "I'll be the Mayor."

The crowd broke out in a roar of applause as The Penguin walked to the window to see the Gotham City skyline. Soon the city would be his — and what would he do with it?

"Burn, baby, burn," he sneered.

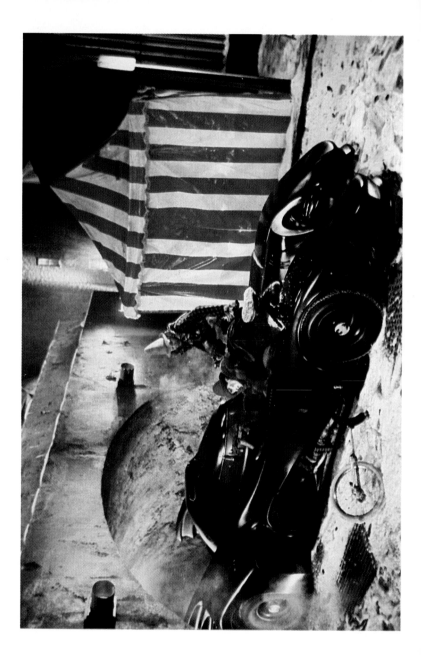

The Red Triangle Circus Gang went to work that very evening. The Organ Grinder blew up an Insta-Teller machine, and, with the aid of his monkey scooped up all the cash. The Flame Thrower torched the ice rink; a group of clowns robbed a pharmacy after writing graffiti on Gotham Plaza's historic statues. The Penguin desperately wanted to join in the fun, but he remained in his warehouse and continued to compile his lists. After all, it wouldn't do for the future Mayor to be seen contributing to the carnage.

On the other side of town, however, Selina Kyle saw no harm in doing her part toward the destruction of Gotham City. As the sounds of explosions, gunshots, and sirens filled the streets outside her apartment, she put on her slinky black costume and leaped out of the window.

In Gotham Plaza, the Knife Thrower was using an ax to smash down a shop door. Around her, other circus members beat defenseless citizens.

Something stirred in the shadows. The circus gang turned to see who, or what, it was.

Batman stood calmly before them. In his hands, he held what at first looked like a portable electronic game machine. As he punched a sequence on the red and white buttons, the Knife Thrower threw a blade straight toward his chest. And although it lodged itself in the Bat-Emblem,

Batman hardly noticed. The thugs rushed toward him as stainless-steel batwings sprouted out of the sides of the device. Then Batman threw the super-Batarang toward the closest gang member.

Like the ball bouncing against the bumpers in a living pinball game, the Batarang careened from thug to thug, slamming them all. Its program complete, the computerized Batarang headed back toward its owner. But before it could complete the preprogrammed course, a ratty poodle leaped up to snatch it out of the air and scurried off with it.

Batman began to chase after the dog, but was stopped by the Sword Swallower. Batman elbowed him in the ribs, and as the Sword Swallower gasped, Batman pulled a sword out of his open mouth. When the Thin Clown with a bomb strapped to his chest came up from behind, Batman sliced the straps and grabbed the bomb. Using the back of the sword, he smashed the Thin Clown down to the pavement.

Selina couldn't remember the last time she had this much fun. Destroying Max Shreck's Department Store was the thrill of a lifetime. In the ladies' evening wear department, she dashed down an aisle, her taloned hand outstretched, slashing the priceless designer blouses on a line of mannequins. She somersaulted onto glass jewelry cases, using her spiked heels to stamp through each and every one. Then she had a *really* neat idea.

Skipping over to the car-care section of the store, she grabbed up an armful of aerosol spray cans and walked over to the housewares department. All those nice microwaves, she thought. She placed a few cans in each machine before turning them all on.

Then she ran.

Outside, Batman came face-to-face with the Tattooed Strongman. "Before I kill you, I let you hit me," the Tattooed Strongman cried. "Come on, hit as hard as you can. I need a good laugh."

Batman figured he was outclassed here. No ordinary punch would faze this guy. But a punch wasn't exactly what Batman planned. He hit the Tattooed Strongman, who responded with a hearty laugh. "You call that a punch?" he bellowed, but he stopped laughing when he looked down at his chest. There, hanging from his leopardskin costume, was the bomb Batman had taken from the clown only moments before.

The Tattooed Strongman attempted to brush it off, but Batman gave him a firm push into a nearby manhole. A moment of silence — and then an explosion boomed out of the manhole.

Batman stared at the plume of gray smoke rising from the manhole and remembered he still needed to find the poodle and retrieve his electronic Batarang. As he turned from the manhole, he noticed The Penguin stepping out of an alley across the street.

Batman watched as The Penguin casually shook some debris off his umbrella and surveyed the burning plaza. When he spotted Batman, he stopped dead in his tracks.

"Admiring your handiwork?" Batman asked.

"Touring the riot scene," The Penguin corrected. "Gravely assessing the devastation. Upstanding mayor stuff."

Batman wasn't amused. "You're not the mayor."

The Penguin shrugged. "Things change," he said. Changing the subject, he offered Batman a hand. "Hey, good to meet you," he said. "We'll be working hand in glove in Gotham's near and glorious future."

Batman didn't shake. Instead, he gestured at the carnage around them. "Once you were their freak. Now they work for you. Must feel pretty good."

"Better than you know, Bat-boy," The Penguin replied smugly.

Batman wasn't in the mood for games. "What're you really after?" he asked.

"Ah, the direct approach." The Penguin smiled. "I admire that in a man with a mask. But you don't really think you'll win . . ."

Batman smiled coldly. "Things change," he said.

The Penguin was about to respond when he heard the sound of shattering glass. He and Batman turned toward Shreck's Department Store in time to see Catwoman crash through the window and perform a series of astounding backflips across the plaza. A final flip, and Catwoman landed on her feet facing them both.

Batman and The Penguin were speechless. Who was this woman with the grace of a cat and a tight leather costume to match?

Catwoman stared them both down. "Meow," she said —

And Shreck's Department Store exploded.

Batman and The Penguin hit the ground as glass and debris rained around them. When the explosion was over, both looked around. Catwoman was gone.

"I saw her first," The Penguin said as he opened his umbrella. "Gotta fly." In an instant, the umbrella's cloth covering fell off, revealing swirling helicopter blades. Before Batman's astonished eyes, The Penguin took off. Batman didn't need to follow. He knew he'd be seeing The Penguin again soon. He wasn't so sure about Catwoman.

Reaching into his utility belt, Batman removed a grappling hook and fired it toward a nearby rooftop. After using it to scale the side of the building, he hopped across the rooftops in search of Catwoman.

"Where's the fire?" she said, slinking down the side of a rooftop power shack. Batman could see her costume was torn in places. He liked the look.

"Shreck's," he began. "You —"

Catwoman suddenly kicked him in the face. Batman

staggered back, then came forward and knocked her to the ground with a single powerful blow. Catwoman looked up, shocked.

"How could you?" she wailed. "I'm a woman!"

Batman was stunned. In all his battles he'd never gotten this sort of reaction. "I'm sorry," he said —

And Catwoman kicked him in the chest, pushing Batman back over the building's ledge. He reached for something to stop his fall, and felt Catwoman's whip coil around his wrist.

After tying her end of the whip to a nearby weather vane, Catwoman leaned over the ledge to watch Batman dangle helplessly. "As I was saying," she continued, "I'm a woman, and can't be taken for granted. Are you listening, you Batman you?"

"Hanging on every word," Batman grimaced.

Catwoman thought that was pretty funny. Very ironic. She appreciated irony and had a few ironic facts of her own. "A man dressed up as a bat is a he-man," she said, "but a woman dressed as a cat is a she-devil."

Now it was Batman's turn to laugh. "A 'he-man'? Sure. They shine that signal in the sky, then wonder what hole I crawled out of." As he spoke, Batman used his free hand to remove a red and blue capsule from his utility belt.

"If you're so down on 'them' out there," Catwoman asked, "why bust your bat-buns to protect 'em?"

"I can't sleep at night," Batman replied, as he squeezed

the tube, forcing the two liquids to mix. "Exploding department stores keep me up."

"I can't sleep either, lately," Catwoman admitted. "A little link between us. But bottom line, baby," she said as she used her talons to begin cutting the whip that held Batman aloft, "you live to preserve the peace, and I'm dying to disturb it. That could put a serious strain on our relationship."

The tube in Batman's hand bubbled purple. It was ready. Before Catwoman could cut through the whip, Batman lobbed the tube up onto the roof, where it exploded against Catwoman's arm. She screamed in pain and, losing her balance, fell over the ledge past Batman. She scraped frantically at the wall as she slid down, trying to get a handhold. Batman leaped down after her and, catching her by the wrist, began to lift her up.

"Who are you?" Catwoman asked. "Who's the man behind the Bat? Maybe he can help me find the woman behind the Cat." With her free hand, she touched his chest armor. "That's not him," she said. Then, finding a soft spot just below Batman's midsection, she continued, "Ah . . . here you are!" Talons extended, Catwoman thrust into Batman's stomach. Batman howled in pain, pushing her away.

She fell. "No-o-o," Batman moaned as he watched her body hurtle toward the ground —

And land safely in a passing dumptruck filled with sand.

"Saved by kitty litter," Catwoman mused as she rubbed her burned arm. "Some date . . ."

Batman rubbed his stomach as he watched the truck and its passenger disappear from view. He'd have to take care of those nasty cuts, he thought. But even though they really hurt, for some reason he didn't seem to mind.

The following day, The Penguin made it official. He gathered all the media at his campaign headquarters. Amid banners that proclaimed "OSWALD MEANS ORDER," and "COBBLEPOT CAN CLEAN IT UP," The Penguin threw his hat into the political arena by announcing that he was running for mayor. He had the petitions already in his possession. All that remained was to decide on a date for the special recall election. Amid a hail of applause and flashbulbs, The Penguin turned and waddled up the stairs to his second-floor retreat.

He was greeted there by one of his clowns. "Hey, Penguin," he began. The Penguin savagely stomped on the clown's shoe. "My name's not Penguin! It's Oswald Cobblepot!" The clown apologized profusely. He only wanted to tell his boss that there was someone in his room waiting to see him. Someone . . . special.

In the corner of The Penguin's room, lounging seductively on his bed, lay Catwoman. He always knew he'd see her again. There was no way she could resist his charms.

"Chilly in here," Catwoman purred, pointing to the air conditioners running at full blast on either side of the bed.

"I'll warm you," The Penguin said as he sat down beside her, a sly gleam in his eye.

"Down, Oswald," Catwoman warned. This was a business visit. "We need to talk. You see, we have something in common." The Penguin smiled hopefully. Catwoman shook her head. "Batman," she said.

The Penguin frowned. "What is it with you two? He's already history. Check it out," he said, pointing to a series of maps and diagrams on a nearby wall. Catwoman rose to get a closer look. They were the Batmobile's blueprints! "We're gonna disassemble his spiffy old Batmobile, then reassemble it as an H-bomb on wheels." The Penguin chuckled. "Yesterday's victor is tomorrow's vapor!"

Bad idea, Catwoman thought. "He'd have more power as a martyr," she explained. "No, to destroy Batman we must first turn him into what he hates most, namely, us."

The Penguin liked the sound of that. "Y'mean, frame him?" he asked. From her silence, The Penguin could tell that was *exactly* what she meant. "Well," he added slowly, "a plan *is* forming . . . a vicious one, involving the loss of innocent life —"

Catwoman cut him off. "I want in," she purred.

The Penguin smiled and extended a slimy flipper for her to shake. "You just got yourself a deal, puss."

Bruce Wayne strolled along the streets of Gotham Plaza. The previous evening, The Penguin had once again appeared on TV. This time, he challenged the Mayor to relight the Gotham Plaza Christmas tree. But Bruce knew the challenge was really directed toward the Batman. It was as if The Penguin was daring him once again to confront his circus crew. Bruce was determined not to give The Penguin the satisfaction. He would attend the Christmas tree lighting, all right. But *not* as Batman. Instead, he'd simply mix into the crowd as Bruce Wayne. And if The Penguin tried anything, he'd be ready.

As he walked past the construction crews and happy shoppers on the plaza, he noticed a woman looking into a shop window. It was Selina. Smiling, he walked over.

Selina stared at her reflection in the shop window. "Why are you doing this?" she asked herself, just as she felt a hand on her shoulder. She turned, startled.

"Selina," Bruce said. "Hi. Didn't mean to —"

"Scare me?" Selina completed the thought. "No, actually, I was just scaring myself."

The two began to walk together, and as they passed the newsstand with headlines that screamed "BATMAN BLOWS IT" and "IT'S A CAT-ASTROPHE," Selina shook her head sadly. "What's the story?" Bruce wondered. "Holiday blues?"

"The news these days . . . weird," Selina admitted. "People looking to superheroes for their peace of mind, and blaming their problems on supervillains, instead of themselves, or at least their spouses."

Bruce agreed. "And it's not even accurate," he said. "I mean, 'Batman blows it'? The guy probably prevented millions in property damage."

Selina understood what Bruce was talking about only too well. "I heard on TV," she added, " 'Catwoman is thought to weigh a hundred and forty pounds.' How do those hacks sleep at night?"

A police barricade prevented them from walking farther. Beyond it, workers were hoisting a huge banner over the stage. In a moment, its message was revealed. "THE RELIGHTING OF THE TREE — TONIGHT AT SEVEN." Bruce and Selina could see the Ice Princess on the stage, rehearsing her act. Selina shook her head. "You're not going to that, are you?" she asked. "The relighting of the tree thing?"

Bruce smiled. "I wouldn't be caught dead," he said. "But," he suggested hopefully, "maybe we'll watch it on TV?"

Selina nodded as Bruce took her hand. A few steps to the sidewalk, and Alfred pulled up in the Wayne limousine, ready to take them both away.

"The tree lights up, I press the button . . . no, wait, I press the button and —"

Through the door of her dressing room, The Penguin could hear the Ice Princess talking to herself. The woman was a total, absolute moron! He turned the doorknob and let himself in.

"Who are you?" the Ice Princess demanded coldly.

"Talent scout," The Penguin answered. The Ice Princess smiled and primped her hair. She was always available for talent scouts, no matter how hideous they looked. She noticed the ratty poodle standing by The Penguin, and the little device in its mouth.

"What is that?" The Ice Princess asked. "A camera or something?"

Not quite, The Penguin thought, as he wrenched it free of the pooch's mouth. He pressed a series of buttons and pointed it at the Ice Princess. "Say cheese," he said. Steel wings sprouted out of the box's sides as the Ice Princess smiled.

She liked this guy, Selina thought. He wasn't like the others. Sure, he was rich — rich was nice — but it was much more than just that. She couldn't say he was normal exactly, but he was a lot like her. He seemed to have a secret side that she wanted to explore, and she bet that he could see her secret side too.

Together they sat on a couch in Bruce's enormous living room, the world's largest fireplace burning before them. It was so warm and toasty in here, so lusciously comfortable . . . but she wasn't certain if the warmth she felt was coming from the fireplace, or from inside her.

She leaned over to kiss Bruce. It just felt right. For a moment, she forgot all about her past. The kiss seemed to go on forever, and might have led to something more, but then Bruce pulled away.

"I . . . ah . . . never fool around on the first date," he said sheepishly.

"Nor I, on the second," Selina responded.

"What're you doing three dates from now?" Bruce asked. They both laughed.

The tension broken, Selina hopped off the couch and walked to the television. "Weren't we going to watch the relighting of the tree?" she asked as she flicked the set on.

A scene of pandemonium filled the screen. "We repeat," a reporter standing amid the terrified crowd said, "the Ice Princess has been kidnapped!" The image shifted to Commissioner Gordon standing in front of the Ice Princess's tent. Was it true, the reporter wanted to know, that Batman himself was a suspect?

"The evidence is purely circumstantial," Gordon insisted. He held up a bag containing Batman's stolen computerized Batarang. "We found this," he said sadly, "stained with blood, in the missing girl's dressing room."

Bruce and Selina were both stunned. For a moment they stood there, both uncertain of how to make their necessary exits. Bruce spoke first.

"I'm, uh, just going to check on those chestnuts Alfred was roasting," he said, and took off. In the next room, Bruce ran into Alfred. He asked the butler to make up some kind of excuse to Selina, something that wouldn't make her hate him, and Alfred smiled. He knew exactly what to say.

As Bruce headed down to the Batcave, Alfred walked toward the living room. He bumped into Selina as she was leaving. As Bruce had done moments before, Selina asked Alfred to make up an excuse for her. Then she awkwardly ran off.

Alone in the mansion, Alfred chuckled. Whatever else may happen, he thought to himself, those two were made for each other.

The Batmobile pulled into the alley unseen. Blocks away, the citizens of Gotham City were milling about the plaza uncertainly. Was Batman a criminal or a hero? Whom would they trust? Whom would they believe? Batman himself wasn't sure, and there was no need to drive the Batmobile into the middle of the plaza to find out. Better to examine the situation from the shadows. Then, unseen by all, he could figure out what The Penguin was up to and stop him permanently.

Once out of the Batmobile, he activated the car's security systems. In an instant, a metal sheath encased the vehicle, locking it tight as a drum. Then he turned and ran off into the shadows.

If only he'd lingered behind a moment, Batman would have seen The Penguin's plan in action. From the other direction, the Red Triangle Circus Gang approached. Each carried a toolbox. Each wore a helmet with a precise drawing of a portion of the Batmobile's blueprints printed on it. And if each managed to make their assigned adjustments to the Batmobile's inner workings, Batman would be in for a very nasty ride home.

The Knife Thrower was first. She climbed atop the Batmobile and, using a small hand-held laser, pried open the security shield. With a whoosh, the shield was gone. The Batmobile stood undefended. Now the real job could begin.

While the circus gang dismantled the Batmobile, Batman stood on a rooftop blocks away. He scanned the crowd, then looked at a building on the opposite side of the street. Through a lit window, Batman could see the bound and gagged Ice Princess. He removed a grappling hook from his utility belt and shot it across the street.

As Batman swung through the air on a mission to save both the Ice Princess's life and his own reputation, the Red Triangle Circus Gang began to make their "adjustments" to the Batmobile. Wires were twisted. Clamps were added. And a special antenna was installed under the chassis of the car. Batman would never see it — and by the time he might realize it was there, it would be too late. When the job was done, the Knife Thrower reactivated the security shield.

Batman was as good as dead.

Batman stood on the window ledge outside the window and peered inside. Except for the Ice Princess strapped to the chair, the room was empty. He heard the sounds of sirens in the street below as he crawled inside and pulled the gag out of the Ice Princess's mouth.

"Gotta hurry," he said as he began untying the many knots that bound the princess. "I was set up to look like I did this —"

"No sweat," the Ice Princess interjected calmly. "I'll just tell the police I was kidnapped by an ugly bird-man with fish breath."

"Did someone say 'fish'?" a voice from above purred. Batman looked up as Catwoman dropped from the ceiling and into the center of the room. She back-flipped past Batman, landing next to the Ice Princess. With a single sweep of her talons, she cut through the princess's ropes. Then she grabbed the princess and dragged her out of the room, slamming the door behind her.

Batman pushed at the door but it was locked. He kicked it open with his boot.

The hallway was empty. But Batman could hear the Ice Princess's cries from above. He raced up the stairs after the sound. An instant later, he was on the rooftop.

Catwoman was gone. Only the Ice Princess remained. She stood on the roof's ledge, shivering in fear. One wrong move, Batman knew, and she'd plunge to her death. He had to be careful.

"Okay," he said, coming closer, "just slowly move toward me . . . away from the edge . . ." The Ice Princess carefully stepped forward.

"Look out!" The Penguin cried out from behind. "Lawn dart!" Batman turned, just in time to see The Penguin hurl an umbrella at the Ice Princess. Batman watched helplessly as it sailed across the roof, embedding itself mere inches away from the princess's foot. An instant later, the umbrella popped open, unleashing a swarm of angry baby bats.

As the Ice Princess swatted at the horrible little creatures, Batman leaped toward her. But it was too late. The Ice Princess stepped back into thin air. And as she fell, she was caught in the glare of one of the spotlights roaming across the plaza. Batman, arms outstretched to save her, was caught in another spotlight.

To the Gothamites staring up in horror, it seemed as though Batman had just pushed the woman to her death. As they watched her fall, they couldn't believe their eyes. Batman? Cold-blooded murder? It couldn't be! But then the Ice Princess reached her final destination: the Christmas tree light button. She slammed into it with full, sickening force and, miracle of miracles, the Christmas tree lit up! And as it did, the thousands of bats The Penguin had planted inside went wild, streaming out into the terrified crowd. To the frightened masses, that clinched it. Batman was a killer. He had to be stopped.

On the rooftop, Batman felt sick. The Ice Princess was dead. Hundreds of people were being terrorized by the bats. And all he could do was watch. No, he corrected himself. There *was* something he could do. He turned to The Penguin. Although it went against his every principle, he actually believed he could kill this evil little man. Batman lunged toward him as the rooftop door burst open to reveal a squadron of armed cops.

Batman paused before them. "Wait!" he pleaded —

A volley of bullets slammed into his armored chest, pushing him back and over the edge of the roof. He fell a moment, then bounced off the side of one terrace, before clanging to rest on a second twenty feet below.

He had to get up, had to get away. Between the bullets and the fall, he was in pretty bad shape. He tried to stand, but found himself being gently pushed back down by Catwoman. As she leaned in close over him, he could see she held a sprig of mistletoe above her head. She kissed him — but cat-style, a long lick over his lips.

"A kiss under mistletoe," he murmured. "Mistletoe can be deadly, if you eat it . . ."

Catwoman smiled. "But a kiss can be even deadlier, if you mean it." Then she lifted Batman up and pressed him against the railing. She poised her talons to claw at his face —

But Batman performed a reverse flip, diving right over

the edge of the terrace. He must be crazy! Catwoman thought — until she looked over the edge and saw Batman floating away. A pair of cloth wings had sprouted from the sides of his body armor.

Catwoman turned from the terrace. The Penguin stood there waiting for her. "You said you were going to SCARE the Ice Princess!" she growled angrily.

"And I kept my word." The Penguin giggled. "The lady looked terrified."

Disgusted, Catwoman tried to leave, but The Penguin held out a small box in front of her. In it was a hideous thing that might have passed for an engagement ring. "Let's consummate our fiendish union," The Penguin suggested, raising his eyebrows suggestively.

Catwoman almost gagged at the thought. "I wouldn't touch you to scratch you, you repulsive . . . awful . . . PENGUIN."

The Penguin's lip trembled with anger. "The name is Oswald Cobblepot," he declared, suddenly reaching out to hook his umbrella handle around Catwoman's neck. It automatically tightened into a noose and lurched upward, its blades rotating like a helicopter. "And the wedding's been called *off*."

Catwoman was yanked into the sky, the handle around her neck strangling her. She saw The Penguin wave a sad good-bye, then disappear from the terrace.

The umbrella-copter carried her high over the city as she struggled against the noose. Finally, she managed to slip her talons under the handle and break free.

Now she was falling, again. She crashed through a skylight window and into a tableful of flowers and soft dirt. She'd landed in a greenhouse of some sort! She lay there for a moment, too stunned by recent events to move. Would every man she ever met eventually try to kill her? What did it take to find a little happiness in this world?

As she howled in frustration and anger, the sound shattered the fragile greenhouse glass.

The Penguin still had one more thing to do. Like a man possessed, he waddled across the plaza to his campaign bus and locked himself inside. There, he sat down in the driver's seat of a miniaturized Batmobile kiddie ride. Its dashboard control panel was filled with switches, buttons, and levers, all identical to the original. It even had a video screen and a mini-steering wheel. Now all The Penguin had to do was sit back and wait for the fun to begin.

After removing the security shield, Batman staggered into the Batmobile, and not a moment too soon. A mob of angry citizens appeared at the end of the alley behind him. When they saw the Batmobile, they raced forward with blood on their minds.

He was about to fasten his seat belt when he heard the door lock. Funny, he thought. I didn't press any buttons.

Then the control panel in front of him lit up. He stared at the dashboard in disbelief. The engine roared to life. What's going on here? Batman wondered.

The video screen next to the steering wheel blipped to life. But instead of Alfred's familiar image, the face of The Penguin filled the screen.

"Don't adjust your set," the video voice cackled. "Welcome to the Oswald Cobblepot School of Driving. Gentlemen, start your screaming."

With a force that pressed Batman back into his seat, the Batmobile took off.

The Penguin could see it all. On one video screen, he watched Batman's tense face. On the other, he could see the Batmobile's point of view. He joggled his miniature steering wheel gleefully. "Maybe this is a bad time to mention it," he said happily, "but my license has expired. Of course," he added, "so have you!"

In the Batmobile, Batman was already at work, trying to regain control of his car before The Penguin crashed it into the Gotham Plaza crowd. He ripped a handful of wires out from the dashboard, reconnecting them to no effect. The dials on the dash continued to spin about crazily, and Batman was powerless to stop them.

"Batman," The Penguin said, "I know you're not having a swell time, but lemme tellya, taking control of your vehicle, mowing down decent people, and laying the bad vibes squarely on you makes the hairs in my nose tingle."

Batman wasn't amused at all, especially when the car

took a turn toward a traffic jam in the center of Gotham Plaza.

The Batmobile plowed into the traffic, knocking cars onto the sidewalk and through store windows as it barreled its way toward the main intersection. There, the Batmobile smashed into a gridlocked auto, sending it flying into a nearby fire hydrant. The car knocked the hydrant clean off, sending a geyser of water up to the electrical wires strung overhead. Sparks fell to the ground, setting a small store aflame.

While Batman continued to tear at the console wires, the Batmobile moved onward toward The Penguin's next target. "Just relax," The Penguin offered, "and I'll take care of the squealing, wretched, pinhead puppets of Gotham."

Take that old lady crossing the street, for example. She was frozen in fear, trapped like a deer in the headlights. The Penguin smacked a button marked "Accelerator," and the Batmobile shot forward. He licked his lips gleefully. "Helpless old lady at twelve o'clock," he announced.

In total desperation, Batman yanked open a ceiling panel, producing another tangle of wires and fuses. With seconds to go, he made a decision and pulled out a round fuse.

The Batmobile squealed to a sudden dead halt, inches away from the old lady. That's it, then, Batman thought. He breathed a sigh of relief —

And the Batmobile surged back to life, tearing off down

the street once again. Batman heard sirens. He turned to look out the back window. A trio of police cars were coming up fast, their guns firing at the Batmobile.

On the video screen, The Penguin was laughing hysterically. "You gotta admit," he said, fighting back tears of joy, "I've played this stinking city like a harp from hell!"

Batman had heard enough. Tightening his hand into a fist, he smashed the video screen. He might have lost control of the Batmobile, but he didn't have to listen to that garbage. Now, at least, he could concentrate.

It didn't take long for him to realize that The Penguin must have been controlling his vehicle with radio waves. And if that was the case, he needed some sort of antenna to transmit his electronic commands. Batman hadn't seen anything suspicious on the roof when he entered the Batmobile, so —

He kicked at the floor of the car, hard enough to dent it. Then he reached over and tore back the floorboard. Beneath another tangle of wires, he could see the Batmobile's gears spinning wildly. Steeling himself, he drove his fist into the gears, hoping his armored glove would protect his hand. The gears squealed as they ground against the glove, but Batman managed to reach through and under the car.

He groped around the bottom of the car and felt the antenna. With a flick of his hand, he snapped it in half.

The Batmobile was suddenly spinning about wildly.

Freed of The Penguin's control, right now there was no one at the wheel. Batman pulled his hand out of the hole and, gripping the steering wheel tightly, stepped on the accelerator. Two police cruisers appeared in his rear-view mirror.

As he fiddled with some wires with his free hand, Batman made a sharp right. The police cruisers followed.

Up ahead, the street became considerably narrower. Narrower, Batman figured, than the Batmobile itself.

The cops in pursuit figured that too. "He'll never fit," one said. So then what could Batman be up to?

In the Batmobile, Batman sparked two wires together. The windshield wipers came on. That wasn't what he'd hoped for. But then, who knew how many "adjustments" The Penguin had made to his car? If Batman was going to get through the alley looming up ahead, his next choice had better be the right one.

He selected another pair of wires and connected them.

The sides of the Batmobile fell away, and the wheels retracted. The Batmobile had transformed into the rollerblade-like Batmissile, and it was now thin enough to scrape through the narrow alleyway.

The police cruisers weren't so lucky. The first became wedged between the two buildings. The second piled into the first.

Seconds later, the Batmissile emerged from the other side of the alley. It performed an angled speed-skate around a corner, and disappeared into the night.

This was it, The Penguin guessed. His moment of triumph. The day he lived for. One more speech, and Gotham City would be his.

Then why did he feel so lousy? Was it because Bat-boy was still alive and well? Maybe. Or because he'd been rejected by Catwoman and was forced to kill her? Possibly. Or was it because, with all of his political wheeling and dealing, he had lost sight of the reason he started this thing in the first place?

Definitely. And he'd have to correct that. Soon.

Right now, however, he'd have to meet the masses for his "Recall the Mayor" rally in Gotham Plaza. Shreck, ever optimistic, accompanied him. "They're ready to bond with you," Shreck said as he led The Penguin toward the stage.

The Penguin wasn't impressed. "We'll celebrate tonight," Shreck offered. "At my Max-squerade ball. Shreck and Cobblepot, the visionary alliance." Sure, sure, The Penguin thought. Whatever you say.

The little man waddled up to the platform, a special black umbrella clenched in his flipper. From below, thousands of citizens cheered him on. Maybe Max was right, The Penguin thought. Maybe being king of Gotham City was enough. He cleared his throat to speak.

"When it came time to ensure the safety of our city," he began, "did the Mayor have a plan? No, he relied on a man. A 'bat' man — a ticking time bomb of a costumed freak who finally exploded last night . . ."

Bruce Wayne clicked off the television. He'd heard just about enough. Now it was time to act. He left the living room and entered the Batcave below Wayne Manor. Standing in front of a computer console, he placed a shiny silver CD onto a platter. Then he flipped a switch. The Penguin appeared on the huge video monitor hanging over the console, still ranting.

"You ask, am I up here for personal glory?" The Penguin squawked. "Ha. I toiled for many years in happy obscurity. No, the glory I yearn to recapture is the glory of Gotham!"

Nearby, Alfred sat at another computer console, where he punched up the "FIND FREQUENCY" command. A moment later the computer responded: "FREQUENCY FOUND." Alfred then pressed another button to begin the "JAM FREQUENCY" command. Another second and the computer blinked: "FREQUENCY JAMMED."

Good, Bruce thought, as he pressed the "PLAY" button on his own machine. It was high time he had some fun.

On the podium in Gotham Plaza, The Penguin had the public eating out of the palm of his hand. They hung on his every word, oohed and ahhed at his every phrase. They were his.

And then his microphone went dead. Strangely, that didn't seem to stop his words from ringing out over the plaza. Only problem was, they were his words to Batman the previous night! "Hey, just relax and I'll take care of the squealing, wretched, pinhead puppets of Gotham," his voice proclaimed proudly.

"Wait a second," The Penguin protested. "I didn't say that!" But he had.

"Ya gotta admit," his voice continued, "I've played this stinking city like a harp from hell!" The Penguin turned left, then right. From both sides, his supporters were backing off the stage, "good old" Max Shreck among them. As the crowd began to boo and hiss, The Penguin made a mental note to design a special fate for his former "visionary ally."

In the Batcave, Bruce Wayne was having a ball. Playing DJ for the moment, he "scratched" the CD, and miles away in Gotham Plaza, the phrase "this stinking city" played over and over again, raising the anger of the crowd to greater heights with each repetition. Soon, the crowd started pelting their former hero with eggs and tomatoes. In response, The Penguin grabbed his special umbrella and pointed it toward the hecklers. And while television cameras recorded his every movement, The Penguin started spraying bullets into the crowd.

That clinched it, The Penguin thought. My political career is over. Kaput. Finito. As the crowd dispersed, he saw a chance to escape with his skin intact. He leaped off the stage and ran toward the park. Behind him, a group of angry citizens followed.

He ran as fast as his little legs could carry him. Up ahead, he saw a bridge that looked familiar — a beautiful storybook affair, with a cheery brook bubbling below. Was this the one? The Penguin wondered. He wanted to get down on his knees and cry.

Instead, he climbed over the bridge and dropped down into the icy waters.

Along the tunnels he floated, retracing the path he'd taken so many years before. At the end of his journey, he found himself in the sewer pipe that led to his old lair. Head held low, he trudged through the slime and filth until he bumped into something familiar. His Duck Vehicle! It would come in handy soon. He climbed aboard and revved the engine, heading toward the abandoned arctic island he once called home.

As he approached, the penguins emerged from their shelter. They squawked and played happily with each other, and The Penguin couldn't help smiling. "My babies," he said. "Did you miss me?" The penguins seemed to squawk that they had.

As The Penguin docked the Duck Vehicle, the remainder of the Red Triangle Circus Gang gathered around.

"Where's my list?" he suddenly shouted at them. "Bring

me the names!" A moment later, the Knife Thrower brought The Penguin's stack of legal pads. He browsed through the names for a moment, then looked up and smiled. "It's time," he said. Then, with dark glee, he added, "Gotham will never forget."

He tore a page off the top of a pad and handed it to one of the clowns. He handed another to the Knife Thrower. Soon, all the members of the gang had a couple of sheets each, but none understood what the names scrawled over the pages meant.

Okay, The Penguin figured. It's time to spill the beans. Fill them in on the plan. "These are the first-born sons of Gotham," he declared. "Like I was! And just like me, a terrible fate waits for them! Tonight, while their parents party, they'll be dreaming away in their safe cribs, their soft beds, and we will snatch them, carry them into the sewer, and toss them into a deep, dark, watery grave!"

One of the acrobats swallowed hard. He didn't like this idea at all. "Umm, Penguin," he began sheepishly. "I mean — kids? Sleeping? Isn't that a little —"

In response, The Penguin raised his umbrella and shot the acrobat dead. "No," The Penguin added darkly. "It's a LOT."

Bruce Wayne wasn't sure why he had come to this party. After all, he and Max Shreck, the party's sponsor, weren't exactly the best of friends. Still, he was feeling pretty good about life in general this evening. He'd managed to expose The Penguin for the foul bird he was and had restored Batman's reputation in the process. The worst seemed to be behind Gotham City now. All that remained was to capture The Penguin and what was left of his gang, and track down Catwoman. He suspected he might be able to reason with her at least.

But still, the question remained: why had he come to Max Shreck's annual Max-squerade Costume Ball, dressed as Bruce Wayne? Deep down, he knew. While everyone around him hid under masks and capes and costumes, he wanted to be seen. But not by the general public. Oh, no. He wanted to be seen by one person in particular. A woman.

Selina.

Their eyes met for a brief moment when she first walked into the room. Like Bruce, she had come dressed as herself, the only other party guest to do so. Chip was about to ask her to dance, when Bruce stepped between them. In a moment, Chip was forgotten, and the two were dancing.

"So," Bruce asked hopefully, "why'd you come tonight?"

"You first," Selina answered.

"To see you."

Selina felt a little uncomfortable now. "That's lovely," she said, "and I really wish I could say the same, but . . . I came for Max."

Bruce was confused. "You don't mean . . . you and Max . . . ?"

Selina laughed and shook her head. "THIS and Max," she said as she pulled a small pistol from her evening bag. Shocked, Bruce pushed the gun back into the bag. "Now, don't give me a killing-Max-won't-solve-anything speech, because it will," Selina insisted. "Aren't you tired of him always coming out on top? When he should be six feet under?"

Part of Bruce agreed. Shreck's plan for the power plant, and his support of The Penguin, had thrown the entire city into chaos. No doubt about it, the man was evil. But still . . . "Selina," Bruce suddenly blurted out, "you're not the judge or the jury. I mean, just who do you think you are?"

Selina shook her head sadly. "I don't know anymore, Bruce," she said, as they danced beneath a sprig of holiday mistletoe. Selina kissed him gently. "A kiss under mistletoe," she said softly. Then she remembered Batman's words. "Mistletoe can be deadly, if you eat it . . ."

Bruce completed the thought. "But a kiss can be even deadlier, if you mean it."

Suddenly it hit them. Could it be? "You're her?" he said, at the same time as she asked, "You're him?"

Bruce tenderly undid the cuff of Selina's sleeve and rolled it up. He didn't need to see it to know. "The burn I gave you," he whispered.

Selina's hand moved under Bruce's shirt, stopping on the bandages. "The puncture wounds I gave you," she gasped. "Oh, God," she said wearily. "Does this mean we have to start fighting now?"

Bruce didn't know what to say. So instead of saying anything, he held her close. "What do we do?" she whimpered.

"I don't know," Bruce admitted. "Till we figure it out, let's . . . let's keep dancing."

Bruce and Selina were about to complete their dance when the floor exploded, and The Penguin, sitting in his Duck Vehicle, burst through. He was accompanied by the Organ Grinder and his monkey, and a quartet of penguins armed with missile launchers.

"You didn't invite me, so I crashed," The Penguin quipped before the dazed and confused group of partygoers.

The Mayor stepped forward as The Penguin jumped off the Duck Vehicle to mingle with the crowd. "What do you want . . . 'Penguin?' " sneered the Mayor.

The Penguin didn't have time for petty name-calling. He had an important announcement to make. He pushed the Mayor aside and began. "Right now, my troops are fanning out across town, for your children," he declared, pausing a moment to let it sink in. "Yes," he assured them, "for your first-born sons, the ones you left defenseless at home, so you could dress up like jerks, get juiced, and dance, badly."

As The Penguin spoke, the Organ Grinder searched through the crowd, looking for one face in particular. Once he found it, the Organ Grinder pointed a gun at the man's head and dragged him back to The Penguin's side. "I've PERSONALLY come for Gotham's favorite son," The Penguin said, motioning to the man at the Organ Grinder's mercy. "Mr. Chip Shreck!"

On the other side of the Duck Vehicle, Selina watched as Chip was hustled on board. Poor Chip, she thought. Even *he* didn't deserve this. "Bruce," she whispered, "We have to do somethi —" But her voice broke off as she turned. Bruce Wayne was gone. Then from near where The Penguin stood, she heard another voice, one she despised almost as much as The Penguin's.

"Not Chip! Please!" Max Shreck begged. "Penguin. If you have one iota of human feeling, you'll take me instead!"

The Penguin smiled. "I don't. So, no." He turned to leave, but Shreck had latched onto his coattails.

"I'm the one you want!" Shreck pleaded. "Penguin, please! Ask yourself — isn't it Max Shreck who manipulated and betrayed you? Isn't it Max, not Chip, whom you want to see immersed to his eyeballs in raw sewage?"

The Penguin rubbed his chin a moment, mulling it over. "Okay," he finally said matter-of-factly. "You have a point." He turned to the Organ Grinder and directed him to let Chip go. The Organ Grinder obeyed. Then he grabbed Shreck roughly and tossed him inside the Duck Vehicle. When Shreck and the Organ Grinder were both on board, The Penguin leaped inside.

And as the Duck Vehicle descended back into the huge hole, the quartet of penguins fired a volley of smoke bombs to make certain they wouldn't be followed.

At last, The Penguin's plan was unfolding, and from all reports, things were going better than even he expected. All across Gotham City, children were disappearing. Being plucked out of cribs, out of nurseries, out of playrooms. Most didn't even put up a fight. After all, what child could resist a happy clown, or the promise of a pony ride? One of his clowns even reported that a kid had mistaken him for the Tooth Fairy!

All those children, The Penguin thought. In an hour or two, there should be thousands of them here, all waiting to walk into his flesh-eating sludge pit. And the best part was, Max Shreck, caged above another slightly less toxic sludge pool nearby, would have to watch each and every child walk to his doom. The Penguin marveled at his good fortune. Sure, it was overdue . . . but better late than never!

The Red Triangle Circus wagons were in bad shape. Their paint had long ago faded from a bright circus red to a drab yellow orange. The circus logo, once proudly painted on the side of each wagon, had long since peeled away. Now, all that remained were the wooden cages and the thick metal bars that ran up and down their exposed sides. Through them, one might catch a disturbing glimpse of a little pair of hands or a little pair of eyes. And if you listened carefully, you might hear the occasional cry of a cold or hungry baby.

But the Organ Grinder paid no attention to any of this as he led the caravan of wagons slowly through the empty Gotham City streets. The pet monkey by his side chittered impatiently as his master barked at the other gang members. "Wouldja hurry up loading those kids already?" What a job. He shook his head in disgust.

A shadow fell across his face. His monkey screamed in terror. He looked up — and Batman yanked the Organ Grinder from the wagon.

A few minutes later, the Organ Grinder's monkey appeared at the top of The Penguin's arctic lair. He was holding something in his hands. "So, where're the kids?" The Penguin demanded as the monkey scampered toward him. He wanted to get this show on the road.

"Boss," the Fat Clown observed, "I think he's got a

note." As if to prove the clown's point, the monkey waved a tiny piece of stationery in his hand. The Penguin snatched it away and read it.

"Dear Penguin," the note began. "The children regret they're unable to attend. Have a disappointing day. Batman." The Penguin crushed the note in his flipper, and raised his umbrella gun at the monkey dancing on the ice before him.

"You're the messenger," he reminded himself. "It doesn't make sense to shoot the messenger."

He turned and shot the Fat Clown instead.

That felt much better, he thought. Now he had to go and speak to some friends.

A few moments later, The Penguin stood before his army of Penguin Commando Bombers. Each wore a communications helmet. Each had a bazooka strapped to his back. The Penguin addressed his team.

"Thanks to Batman, the time has come for us to punish ALL God's chillun — first, second, third, and fourth born. Male AND female. Why be biased?" If he was expecting an answer, he would have been disappointed. The penguins stood motionless, like zombies awaiting a command.

So The Penguin gave one. "Forward march!" he cried. "The liberation of Gotham has begun!" In unison, the penguin army swiveled and waddled toward the big open sewer pipe.

The Penguin dried the tears from his eyes as he watched them go.

There was more than one way to track The Penguin, Batman thought as he hurtled through the sewer in his Batskiboat. Half speedboat, half jet-ski, the sleek black vehicle was every bit as technically advanced as the Batmobile and Batplane.

The Gotham City sewer system was far too complicated to ever find The Penguin by traditional means. But Batman had an extra advantage. He knew how The Penguin worked — and he had a few tricks of his own. All he needed was to find one group of the armed penguins —

And there they were, up ahead.

The penguins' headgear clicked and whirred as they watched the Batskiboat approach. Electronic impulses were relayed back to their lair, where The Penguin's computers could analyze the target before issuing a fire command. If the Batskiboat's computer could lock on the signal, Batman could follow it right to The Penguin's hideout.

The Batskiboat twisted suddenly, climbing the sewer walls, narrowly avoiding the penguins in its path. As it left the penguin squadron behind, Batman looked at his computer console and smiled. "I'm homing in on the signal's origin," he announced.

Miles away, in the Batcave, Alfred sat at the console he'd used to jam The Penguin's speech the day before. He was ready to give it another try. "Ready when you are, sir," he said.

A few moments later, and he was. Batman's on-board computer had determined the exact location of The Penguin's lair. Now the Batskiboat had a true destination.

Before he could reach it, however, he had to get past another pair of penguins directly in front of him. As he angled his vehicle away, they fired their payloads. The bazooka shells blasted toward their target, and Batman needed to turn all the way to avoid them. Before he realized it, the Batskiboat was cruising on the sewer tunnel's ceiling, passing over the heads of the penguins down below. As the two missiles exploded harmlessly behind him, Batman pressed onward.

Watching his army from his video computer terminal, The Penguin still hadn't given up hope. Batman might have avoided two of his Penguin Commando divisions, but he'd completely overlooked the largest and deadliest division. Right now, they were heading toward Gotham Plaza — and nothing could stop them from blowing the place to smithereens!

But in the Batcave, Alfred received the last of the signal coordinates relayed to him by Batman. With this information, he could not only trace the signal, but control it as well. "Shall we?" Batman asked.

"Let's dance, sir," Alfred answered, pressing a button. In an instant, the words "FREQUENCY JAMMED" appeared on the screen.

On the outskirts of Gotham Plaza, the penguins' headgear began to whine and rattle. Then the entire group turned and trotted away from the plaza.

In his lair, The Penguin was glued to his video screen. He savored the image of Gotham Plaza — once his penguins were done with it, it would never look quite the same. He waited for the torpedoes to fire, but the moment never came.

The Poodle Lady at the computer controller sounded nervous. "F-funny thing, your p-penguins," she stammered. "They're not responding to the launch command. In fact, they're kind of turned around now . . . like someone jammed our signal."

"But who could've —?" The Penguin's eyes flared with anger. "No," he cautioned the Poodle Lady. "Don't say it."

"My lips are sealed," she answered.

The Penguin rose from the video screen and, after

grabbing the nearest umbrella, jumped into the Duck Vehicle, steering it out of the lair and up the stairs.

Was this luck or what? Max Shreck thought as the Organ Grinder's monkey chittered about in front of his cage. The disgusting little creature has a key! Reaching over, Shreck grabbed it and quickly unlocked his cage. With The Penguin gone, there was nothing to stop him from escaping. As he prepared to step carefully from the cage to the ground, Catwoman's bullwhip suddenly wrapped around him. It jerked him violently out of the cage, and sent him splashing into the water below. As the bullwhip slowly pulled Shreck out of the icy sludge, he noticed the Fat Clown floating lifelessly next to him — and spotted the gun dangling from the clown's body. Without hesitation, he snatched it away; he suspected he might be needing it soon.

Thanks to Alfred and the computer in the Batcave, Batman finally knew where he was going. The coordinates confirmed it: The Penguin's base of operations was the lowest level of the old Arctic World Pavilion in the abandoned Gotham City Zoo. Time to meet him face to face and wrap this game up.

Then Batman noticed the unusual duck-shaped image on his radar screen. It could be only one thing. The

Penguin was on the move again. If he lost track of him now, he might never find him again.

Batman examined the Duck Vehicle's coordinates. If he read them right, they indicated The Penguin was still inside Arctic World, but was rapidly moving up from the underground exhibit area to the ground level.

Batman looked ahead. In the distance, the tunnel forked. One tunnel led straight ahead, while the other angled up toward the surface. He floored the engine, and at the last second steered up.

On the ground level of Arctic World, The Penguin was almost home free. Soon, he'd find a new place to live and a new gang to lord over. One of these days he'd see his dreams come true. For now, he'd just better lie low.

As the Duck Vehicle took the last few steps to freedom, a shadow passed over it. The Penguin looked up, horrified, to see the Batskiboat tear through the top of Arctic World — and crash on top of the Duck Vehicle.

For a moment, there was only silence. Then the canopy of the Batskiboat popped open, and Batman emerged. He looked inside the Duck Vehicle for some sign of The Penguin — but it was empty.

Batman was confused — until The Penguin leaped onto his back, and began clawing at him. Batman managed to shake the bird-man off his back. The two stared at each other. The Penguin held his sword umbrella. Batman produced a small box with a button on it. It was a standoff.

But then, over Batman's shoulder, The Penguin saw something that made him want to cry. "My babies . . . ," he sighed. Batman turned to see the Penguin Commandos. Now obeying a new set of remote control commands, they had returned home. They paused at the entrance to the zoo, awaiting their next order.

As Batman turned to look, The Penguin lunged, jarring the box out of Batman's hand. The Penguin snatched it up and greedily pressed the button —

And a panel in the Batskiboat fell away, releasing a family of bats. They billowed out and flapped straight at The Penguin.

The Penguin tried to fight them off, but there were too many. They sent him smashing through a glass observation window and back into the moat that surrounded the arctic exhibition area.

Batman looked down. There was no sign of The Penguin. But nearby, on the arctic island, Batman could see Catwoman struggling with Shreck. He'd be down there in a second.

First, he'd have to take care of the penguins. He moved back to the Batskiboat and radioed Alfred. He told the butler to stop jamming the penguins' signals and to order them to launch their missiles.

Batman watched as the penguins' headgear began to whir and click again. Then their bazookas were redirected toward the remains of the old zoo. In unison, the penguins fired.

Batman watched as the missiles soared overhead before blowing the remains of the zoo to pieces.

Down on The Penguin's icy arctic island, the world was caving in. The exhibit's air-conditioning generator sputtered and sparked. Huge pieces of flaming debris fell from the sky, melting the ice and warming the water around it. The temperature was rising.

Max Shreck was desperate. Catwoman wanted him dead, and he couldn't, for the life of him, understand *why*. He offered her anything she wanted. Money. Jewels. Even a huge ball of string. But she insisted on one thing alone: his blood.

From up above, Batman suddenly appeared. Max crawled over the ice toward him, begging for help. "You're not just saving one life," he pleaded. "You've saving a city and its WAY of life."

In response, Batman kicked Shreck into the generator. Sparks flew as he jerked against the machine before pitching forward in agony. As he lay gasping for breath, Batman confronted him.

"First, you're going to shut up," Batman demanded. "Then you're going to turn yourself in."

"Don't be naive," Catwoman interrupted. "The law

doesn't apply to people like him! *Or* us —"

"Wrong on both counts," Batman said, grabbing Shreck. Catwoman couldn't allow him to do that. No matter what the cost, she couldn't let Shreck escape justice, *her* justice. She swatted Batman aside and turned toward Shreck.

"Why are you doing this?" Batman pleaded as he rose to his feet. "Let's just take him to the police, then go home together." Catwoman stood still for a moment. She was considering it. "Don't you see," Batman continued as he stepped alongside Catwoman, "we're the same . . . split down the middle . . . *please* . . ." He raised his hands to his head and removed the cowl covering his face. Batman was gone now. It was Bruce Wayne who begged her to listen to reason.

Catwoman was touched. "Bruce, I could live with you in your castle forever. Just like in a fairy tale." As she leaned forward to kiss him, Bruce raised his hands to her face to remove her mask. Suddenly defensive once again, Catwoman spun around and kicked Bruce aside. "I just couldn't live with myself," she said, now resigned to her fate. "So don't pretend this is a happy ending."

"Selina!" Bruce cried out in desperation as she turned back toward her prey. In response, Shreck pulled out the Fat Clown's gun and pointed it at her. Then, in a flash, it came to him: "Selina!" he sputtered. "Selina Kyle? And Bruce — Bruce Wayne! Why are you dressed up as Batman?"

Selina looked at her former boss with contempt. "He IS Batman, you moron."

Shreck raised the gun toward Batman. "Was," he said. And fired.

The bullet nicked Batman's neck. As he hit the ground, Shreck trained the gun on Catwoman.

"You killed me," Catwoman purred as she sauntered toward Shreck. "Batman killed me, The Penguin killed me. Three lives down. Got enough bullets to finish me off?"

"One way to find out," Shreck said, firing a bullet into her arm. And then another, which hit her leg.

She tore off her mask as she continued. "Four, five," she said. "Still alive."

Too dizzy to stand, Batman cried out for her to stop, but she wasn't listening. A third bullet smashed into her other leg, while a fourth shot her hand.

"Six, seven," Catwoman continued. "All good girls go to —"

Shreck pulled the trigger again. It clicked. He was out of bullets.

"Hmm," Catwoman said. "Two lives left. Think I'll save one for Christmas."

Shreck whimpered as Catwoman backed him toward the generator. "What're you—" he cried out, as Catwoman embraced him, pushing them both against the side of the machine. She leaned forward to kiss Shreck, and plunged her steel talons into a pair of open fuseboxes.

Their bodies buckled and jerked together for a few moments, before both were lost under a shower of sparks and smoke.

A thick warm mist hung in the air above the steaming remains of the arctic island. Batman wiped the sweat from his brow as he searched for Catwoman's body, but could find only Shreck's. Was it possible? he thought, stumbling back. Might she still be alive? One thing was certain: she wasn't here.

But someone else was.

The Penguin rose up from the misty waters, soaked and bleeding and gasping for breath. Slowly, he waddled toward the shorted-out generator, using a pair of umbrellas to hold him up. "Gotta crank the A.C.," he wheezed. "Stuffy in here." He twiddled some dials, dropping one of his umbrellas. But the generator was dead. He kicked it once before turning away to face his enemy.

Bruce Wayne's face stared out from above the Batman costume. He looked at The Penguin with contempt.

"Without the mask, you're drop-dead handsome," The Penguin wheezed. "So drop dead."

He raised the umbrella and fired it. It played a little tune. "Heh," The Penguin chuckled through his pain. "Picked the cute one. Heat's getting to me." He reached for the other umbrella lying on the ground — but Batman grabbed it first. "Hey," The Penguin said nervously, "You wouldn't blow away an endangered bird —"

Without a word, Batman raised the umbrella and aimed it between The Penguin's eyes. The Penguin rose and turned, staggering away. "You wouldn't shoot me in the back, wouldya?" Batman remained silent, but kept the umbrella aimed at The Penguin.

With great difficulty, The Penguin staggered toward the once-icy moat. A single chunk of glistening ice rested near the shore. "I'm overheated is all," he wheezed. "I'll murder you momentarily . . . but first, a cool drink . . ." He flopped to the ground, mere inches from his destination. ". . . of ice water . . ."

The Penguin was dead.

Batman lowered the umbrella and stared at his defeated enemy for a moment. From somewhere far off he heard the sound of scuffling feet. He looked to see four huge penguins move out of the shadows toward The Penguin. They surrounded their fallen brother and used their beaks to lift him up onto their shoulders. Together, they carried him back into the shadows.

It was over at last.

As Alfred steered the Rolls-Royce through Gotham Plaza, Bruce Wayne stared out the window. Everything was as it had been. Everything had returned to normal. From the shop windows, to the Christmas tree itself, it was as though nothing had ever happened, nothing had ever changed.

But if that was so, Bruce asked himself, why did he feel this terrible ache in his heart?

"I didn't find her," he said aloud. "Maybe . . ."

"Yes," Alfred answered, wanting only to comfort his master. "Maybe." Alfred turned the car off the main street and onto a shortcut alleyway. As it cruised through the narrow street, Bruce noticed the shadow of a woman cast against the alley wall by the car's headlights. Could it be? Was it — her?

"Alfred, stop!" Bruce cried out, as he blinked in disbelief. He glanced at the shadow again, but now it looked more like a cat than the woman he loved. Still, he had to be certain.

Leaving the car behind, Bruce walked into the alley and searched amid the trash cans for some sign of Catwoman. After a moment, he heard a rustling sound from behind.

It was only a cat, after all. A black cat. It stared at Bruce a moment. Bruce smiled and picked it up before heading back to the car.

"Well," Alfred said as he started the engine, "come what may . . . Merry Christmas, Mr. Wayne."

"Right. Sure." Bruce answered. "And, 'Peace on earth, Goodwill toward men.'"

Bruce looked at the cat purring contentedly in his lap.

"And women," he added.